SNO
THE R

BY THE SAME AUTHOR

Snotty Bumstead

SNOTTY AND THE RENT-A-MUM
Hunter Davies

Illustrated by
Paul Thomas

RED FOX

A Red Fox Book

Published by Random House Children's Books
20 Vauxhall Bridge Road, London SW1V 2SA

A division of Random House UK Ltd
London Melbourne Sydney Auckland
Johannesburg and agencies throughout the world

1 3 5 7 9 10 8 6 4 2

First published in Great Britain by The Bodley Head 1993

Red Fox edition 1994

Set in Plantin

Printed and bound in Great Britain by
Cox & Wyman Ltd, Reading, Berkshire

RANDOM HOUSE UK Limited Reg. No. 954009

ISBN 0 09 929611 X

Contents

To Fred and Edward,
my Carlisle United friends

I

Snotty and the Milkman

It had been one of those long boring days which schools specialize in: non days, in which nothing happens. Each hour, each minute, each second lasted for ever, so it seemed to Snotty, but now that it was over the day was slowly sinking out of sight, ready to join all those other millions and trillions and squillions of school days from the past which have all been forgotten.

"Going, going, going . . ." said Snotty to himself, closing his eyes. He had left the noise and squalor of Camden High Street and was nearing the quieter, more dignified if rather run-down terrace where he lived. It was part of his ritual every Friday, when another week was in the bag, down time's plughole, to close his eyes on the home stretch, walk with one foot in the gutter and at the same time swing his Spurs bag round his body. This was to ward off any creatures from outer space who might be about to fly down and attack him, any beasts from under the earth who might be about to rise up and eat him or, most horrible of all, any stupid

Arsenal fans who might be lying in wait with a leg outstretched.

Two monster Fourth-Year youths, each about seven feet high, shaven heads, boots the size of goal posts, with six bellies between them, appeared across Snotty's path. They looked like giant whales, out searching for plankton, or First Years, whichever might be the smaller. Snotty froze, then melted into the gutter, disappearing out of sight, or so he hoped. They sailed on, oblivious of minor plant life, attending only to their Walkmen.

"I bet they're on steroids," thought Snotty. "Or double All Bran. If only their brains had grown as much as their bodies."

He never said this sort of thing to their faces at school, not being daft, not wanting to provoke them. Snotty's aim in the playground was to keep a profile so low that he would appear flat and therefore non-existent, part of the tarmac landscape.

That afternoon, at break, three even bigger, cleverer, smarter kids, all Sixth Formers, had grabbed him in a corridor and cross-examined him about "accommodation possibilities". Snotty had acted dumb, saying nothing, managing to wriggle out of their sight and into his own classroom.

Miss Eager, his class teacher, she'd also been a pain all day. She'd said his work sheets were messy, his homework late once again, but he was not unduly worried. He was beginning to feel he could deal with her. Deep down, it was obvious, she quite liked him. So Snotty liked to think. Anyway, tonight he would get Sluke to do his homework for him, in his best joined-up writing. Sluke owed Snotty a few favours. Probably ten thousand, at the last count.

Mrs Potter was more of a worry. She was Head of St Andrew's Road Comprehensive and a very busy woman, running a school with fourteen hundred pupils and one hundred staff. Or was it the other way round? Snotty could never remember. Compared with his primary school, it was like being in a jungle.

"Dunno why she's after me," said Snotty to himself, still swinging his bag. "If I was Head, I'd be too busy bossing around one hundred staff. I wouldn't be bothered with any of the boring pupils."

Snotty had met Mrs Potter's secretary just as he was leaving the school gates. She had asked him about his mum: was she OK, was she in good health? Snotty knew the secretary by sight, but he had always assumed she could not possibly know him. Had he not kept his head down for almost two terms? She must be secret police, or a witch. What a cheek! Asking about his mum. She'd actually stood in front of him, waiting for his reply. He'd given her his usual mumbles, put on his best glazed look. It appeared to satisfy her.

Slowly and surely, as Snotty reached his own street, all the aggravations of the school week began to disappear. Very soon his other life would take over. His lovely house, arranged for his pleasure. His lovely evening meal, also arranged for his pleasure, when and how he liked it. It was a secret world, known to nobody at school. Apart from Sluke, his best friend, and of course Bessie and Jessie, his other best friends. No one else knew about Snotty's secret life. As far as Snotty was aware. If anyone ever found out, that would be it.

"Going, going, going," repeated Snotty, still to himself, his eyes closed, carefully counting out his footsteps.

"GONE!" yelled Snotty.

He gave a final twirling, whirling swing to his bag, sending it as far above his head as possible. This was a sign that he had at last banished for ever the moans and groans, the slings and arrows of another draggy week. He was on home territory.

At once he could feel his body relaxing, his mind easing, his face, if only just, taking on its smiling mode. At school, Snotty liked to think he offered a blank face to the world. He believed no one in authority knew he existed. He was a spy, going under cover, trying not to register on their consciousness. Now he was about to become a real human being once again.

There was a strange sensation of weightlessness in his arms. This was unusual, not his normal Friday coming-home feeling. Had some form of extrasensory perception taken over, now that he had thrown away the shackles of the day? He opened his eyes, trying to work it out, looking up into the heavens. His precious Spurs bag had totally disappeared.

"Oh, bloody hell."

"Language!" said Mrs Cheatham, his next-door neighbour, hurrying past him, giving a little shudder as if not wanting to associate with him, but a few steps ahead she paused, unable to resist another chance to tell him off.

"Yes, you are observant," sneered Snotty to himself. "I was using language. Not talking Algebra. Or talking Basic. Have a house point."

Mrs Cheatham glared at him, not quite understanding what he'd said, then she marched on, disappearing up the steps into her own house.

The street appeared deserted. No sign of people, or of his bag. Snotty looked in the gutter, just in case anyone might be crouching there, such as Arsenal fans, the gutter being their natural home, ha ha, he said to himself, without smiling.

At the other end of the street, Snotty noticed that the milkman had parked his float half on the pavement. Mrs Cheatham was usually alert to this crime, getting up petitions, considering it a hanging offence, but today she had missed it.

Snotty narrowed his eyes. Only that day, he'd learned in biology that this does help you to see better, thanks to the retina letting in more light, or is it more dark. Anyway, by straining both eyes he could clearly see that hanging from the top of the milk float's frame was his Spurs bag. It must have twirled itself round the strut, while his eyes were closed; then the float must have moved off silently, being electrically powered, without him hearing it.

"Give us back my stuff!" shouted Snotty.

He'd raced down the street and had now shoved his head angrily into the milk float.

"Excuse me," said the milkman vacantly, without looking up, sucking a pencil and studying his order book.

"I want it back at once!" Snotty was in a mild temper tantrum, the sort he'd often had when he was little, stamping both his little feet.

"Did I hear shouting?" said the milkman calmly, still writing.

"Your stupid milk van has stolen my bag!"

"Try a citizen's arrest," said the milkman. "Feel free to take my milk float into custody if you must, but I'd be obliged if you could wait till I've finished this round, if you don't mind."

"My rotten bag, it's caught up in the top of your thingy, and I can't get it down," said Snotty.

"I suppose we could wait," said the milkman, putting down his pencil, "till you've grown big enough to get it down by yourself, but that might mean a long wait, perhaps for ever . . ."

"Ha ha," said Snotty. That was the sort of infantile remark he had to put up with from Fourth Years all day long, the sort of cheap jibes he didn't expect from an adult, or someone pretending to be an adult. The milkman had always appeared a bit stupid to Snotty, though his mother had always liked him.

"So what happened, Snotty, my petal?" said the milkman smiling. "Tell it slowly. In words of one syllabub . . ."

"I was coming home from school, right, minding my own business, right, my eyes were closed, right, no no, not closed, I was just finking, yeh, working out this stupid homework we have to do, when all of a sudden . . . *ouch!*"

The milk float had moved forward, suddenly but silently, almost running over Snotty's right foot, his best foot, the one with which he had scored fifteen indoor goals (and that was only last night's match).

"Stop messing around," yelled Snotty, running to keep up with the float. "You've got my bag. Up there. Look!"

In his mirror, the milkman looked where Snotty was pointing. He stopped the float and got out.

"Why didn't you tell me the single most vital, most mega, most sonic, most stratospheric fact about your bag, you dum dum . . ."

"What's that?" asked Snotty, as the milkman stretched up and got down his bag.

"Tott-ing-ham, Tott-ing-ham!"

The milkman was swinging Snotty's bag above his head and going through a selection of Spurs chants, as heard on the terraces, some of them not repeatable in respectable company. Snotty could see the imprint of Mrs Cheatham's upturned nose, flat and squashy and wrinkled, as she watched from behind the net curtain of her basement window.

"If only you'd told me you were a Spurs fan," said the milkman, handing Snotty his bag and getting back into his milk float.

"Thanks," said Snotty.

"No problem," said the milkman, driving away. Then he slowed down and stuck his head out.

"But there could be one problem for you," he continued. "I haven't been paid for three weeks. If I don't get the money tomorrow, you could be for it, my lad . . ."

Oh no, thought Snotty, just as things were going so well, just as he was looking forward to a great weekend, just as he was about to get safely inside his own house.

If he couldn't pay the milkman's money, his Big Secret would come out. Then Snotty's world might totally collapse . . .

2

It was 29–29 in the Spurs-Arsenal final. Snotty had scored all the goals for Spurs so far, and taken every throw in, free kick and penalty. He had organized the tactics and made every refereeing decision. Well, it was his game, his pitch, his house. Jessie, the only other member of his team, who was playing goalie, felt pleased to be on his side, as they were bound to win. They usually did. Snotty was also in charge of the score.

Around the walls he had chalked up previous scores, going back now for weeks and weeks.

Sluke and Bessie were playing for Arsenal, and doing very well, considering that Bessie was really a Spurs fan, and considering the odds stacked against them, such as Snotty's habit of creating new rules when it suited him.

"Off the fridge counts as in," shouted Snotty, watching his own shot bounce off three walls, hit the fridge and sneak under Bessie's body. He then did a lap of triumph round the whole of the pitch, cheering himself all the way.

While he was still celebrating, Sluke got the ball, dribbled up field, and took a shot at Jessie. He stubbed his toe on a floorboard, sending the ball straight up in the air, but by luck he managed to collect it when it bounced down, despite not wearing his spectacles, and hammered it in.

"That hit the ceiling," yelled Snotty, as Sluke went off on his own lap of honour. "No goal."

"You said the ceiling was part of the field of play," protested Sluke, a tall, thin, gangling boy. He threw himself down on the floor, saying he was fed up with Snotty changing the rules.

"Yeh, but not that part of the ceiling," said Snotty. "Put your specs on, Four Eyes. You hit that rose thingy."

This was an elaborate piece of plasterwork in the middle of the ceiling, highly decorated, part of the original Victorian house. Snotty was not worried about doing it any artistic damage. The problem was that bits of it were now starting to fall, getting in people's eyes, such as Snotty's, when he was about to score.

"OK then, I'll count that as in," said Snotty. "As I'm in a good mood. That's thirty-thirty. Half-time. We'll have the refreshments now."

Sluke got up off the floor at once and opened the fridge. All it contained were cans of Coke, filling every shelf. He handed out two to each player, then three to himself, as he was extra exhausted.

"Ah, this is the life," said Snotty.

"Wish we had a pitch like this," said Sluke.

"Wish we had a house like this," said Jessie.

"Wish we had a pitch *and* a house like this," said Bessie.

The whole ground floor of Snotty's house had been converted into an indoor football pitch, all furniture and carpets removed, all paintings taken from the walls and, while play was in progress, all windows shuttered from the inside. The kitchen sink had been boarded up and the freezer and the dishwasher put in the basement. Snotty no longer needed to wash dishes, or wash anything. "When all you eat is take-away, all you do is throw-away." That was one of Snotty's favourite new sayings.

Only the fridge had been retained, and proved very useful. Not just for emergency rations but for shooting practice when Snotty was on his own, waiting for the others to come round for their evening match.

The ground floor had been made open-plan many years ago by his mother, which was fortunate, but Snotty had had to organize a bit of extra building work, enlarging the gap between the kitchen and the living room. Sluke had done that, being bigger and marginally stronger than Snotty, but Snotty had provided the hammer, plus instructions, comments, jeers.

"Just gonna play a few machines," said Jessie, getting up, still holding her Cokes.

"Yeh, think I'll listen to something groovy," said Bessie.

Jessie went upstairs to the first floor which had been completely rearranged as a GAMES area, filled with Space Invaders, computer games, video games, electronic toys and remote-controlled cars. There was also a large snooker room which had previously been a bathroom, Snotty's mother's pride and joy. The bath had been covered over with a snooker table. Snotty no longer had baths, and intended never to have one again, so there was no need to have an old-fashioned, stupid, pointless bathroom.

The top floor was devoted to MUSIC: either listening to it, with the help of stereos, jukeboxes, CD players and endless loudspeakers, or trying to create music. Snotty had bought an electric guitar, mail-order of course, and a large drum kit, also mail-order. So far, he had still not managed to put the drum kit together.

"Come on down, you two," shouted Snotty. "Winning goal."

"You said it was half-time," said Sluke. "That means we should play the same length of time as the first half. If we're just playing to the winning goal, that means we'll be finished in no time."

"Don't be a pavement," said Snotty.

"I think you mean pedant," said Sluke.

"I mean pavement," said Snotty. "Just right for jumping on." Which he did, landing on Sluke's back. They rolled over on the floor.

"Oh, no, it's not wrestling now, is it?" said Bessie.

"Right, it's our turn to be strikers," said Jessie, picking up the ball. "You two are goalies, when you've stopped messing around."

Sluke and Snotty finished their wrestling, then got up and went in goals, cheering on their respective strike forces. Bessie scored first, putting Arsenal in the lead, and therefore the winners, but Snotty changed the rules yet again, saying it was first to forty.

They played for another hour, finishing with the score fifty-fifty, an honourable draw.

"I'm knackered," said Sluke, collapsing on the floor. Somehow he managed to crawl a few metres across the floor, just making the fridge and getting himself another Coke.

"I saw that," said Snotty. "Pass them round, you greedy beggar."

They all lay on the floor, exhausted, sipping their drinks in a contented silence.

"Any word from your mum?" asked Jessie at length.

"No. Why should there be?" said Snotty, rather sharply.

"Just wondered, you know, if she's safe."

"Course she's safe," said Snotty. "She'd tell me if she wasn't."

Sluke lay on his back, examining the ceiling rose, trying to work out the logic in Snotty's remark. He decided to say nothing. The whole subject of Snotty's mum was very complicated, and very cloudy. He did not want to enquire too much. He wanted her to be safe, of course, but he didn't want her to return, not just yet, when it was so brilliant, so marvellous, being able to play every evening in Snotty's house.

Snotty's mum had brought Snotty up by herself, having separated from Snotty's father many, many years ago. In the past she had often gone off for a few days on location, as she worked in the film world, leaving Snotty with an au pair or a baby-sitter.

Several weeks ago she had had to go off suddenly on a secret and very hush-hush project. Snotty was now older, First Year Comprehensive, so she hoped he'd cope on his own. She'd left him some money, her credit cards, and a note telling him to use her cards to pay the bills. He was "in charge of the house" with a mission "to enjoy himself".

After the first two weeks on his own, with no word from his mother, Snotty had started to re-organize the house on the lines she had clearly suggested (Snotty decided) so that he could enjoy himself.

There had been one phone call from her, and one letter, not saying much, but reassuring Snotty she was alive and well. The letter, sent from somewhere in Africa, was pinned up on the wall beside the football scores. It said she was sending him some tickets, but they hadn't come yet.

The only real problem was that various busybodies, such as Mrs Cheatham next door, and Mrs Potter, his Head Teacher, were becoming convinced that all was not well, that something funny was going on, that a boy of Snotty's age should not be left in that big house on his own.

The other more pressing problem was that Snotty had promised to take them all to Marine Ices, once the match was over, but he suddenly realized he had run out of cash.

3

Jessie and Bessie were standing on either side of the Midland Bank corner, keeping a look-out, ready to give the warning sign, should anyone or anything untoward happen.

Sluke was wearing a long coat and an old trilby hat, both found on a skip. He was standing right in front of the cash-dispensing machine, his arms out wide, hoping to make himself and his coat look as big as possible. In front of him, like a baby kangaroo in a pouch, was Snotty, stretching up, trying to put his mother's bank card into the slot.

"Hurry up," hissed Sluke. "You haven't forgotten the PIN number, have you?"

"Don't be stupid," said Snotty.

He was useless at remembering most things mathematical, but he had memorized his mother's number. After all, he had been using it every weekend for some time now. He never took too much cash out at any one time, just in case he got mugged or burgled, only enough for the week ahead. Any urgent items for the house, vital things like the latest computer-programmed jukeboxes, another Nintendo, or a fourth TV, he bought over the phone by VISA card, quoting his mother's number.

"There's something wrong with this stupid machine," said Snotty.

"There's something wrong with stupid you," said Sluke.

"Belt up, Four Eyes."

"Shurrup, shorty."

"Heh, you two," hissed Jessie, watching them from the corner. "Stop squabbling."

"Not my fault," said Snotty. "This machine. The card keeps on coming back out again. I dunno why. I'll try it one more time . . ."

Just as he was about to put it in, he felt a body landing on top of him, a young, muscular body, fresh from a hard game of indoor football. It was Jessie. In one action, she had knocked him flat and taken the card from his hand.

"You're going to lose it, you idiot," she said. "They only reject it so many times, then they keep it."

"How was I to know," said Snotty, getting up. "And that hurt."

"So what we gonna do?" said Sluke. "I'm starving."

"This is more important than your rotten stomach," said Jessie, examining the card. "You did use the right PIN number, Snotty?"

"I'm not a complete idiot," said Snotty.

"Yes, just an incomplete idiot," said Sluke.

"Shurrup, you," said Snotty.

"Of course," said Jessie, looking at her digital watch, "now I get it."

"Is the bank closed, then?" asked Snotty.

"No, it's the date. Look, it says it's only valid till the thirtieth of the sixth. That was yesterday. You'll have to get a new one."

"How do I do that?" asked Snotty.

"I'm not sure," said Jessie.

"Oh, no," said Sluke. "What we gonna eat?"

"How we gonna *live*?" said Snotty. "That's much more important. Everything will collapse if I can't get any more cash out."

"I think my stomach's collapsing," said Sluke. "I'll probably get anorexia and fade away . . ."

He looked at his own watch. Not to check the date but the time, in the hope that he might get back to his own house for supper. Snotty went on moaning.

"I need cash to buy food, to buy Coke, to buy cereals, all that sort of stuff. It's gonna ruin everything . . ."

"I think I'll have to go," said Sluke. "I promised my mum I would be home tonight. She's getting a bit worried, you know, about me being out all the time . . ."

"Good riddance," said Snotty. "You're no help at all."

"Actually, we have to go as well," said Jessie and Bessie together. "But don't worry, Snotty. We'll think of something. We're bound to find a solution. We'll come round to your place tomorrow morning. OK? Byee."

"Ugh," said Snotty, turning away, feeling very miserable.

Half-way home he remembered what was happening tomorrow morning.

"The milkman! That's all I need. He said he wanted paying tomorrow morning. Or else. Oh, no . . ."

4

Snotty, Sluke, Jessie and Bessie were all sitting on Snotty's indoor football pitch, having ice-cream for breakfast, as they did most Saturday mornings. In the old days, Snotty's mother had made him a fry-up on Saturday, followed by croissants, which Snotty had quite liked, but he much preferred ice-cream. Especially now he had his own supply, made on the premises, without him having to do any work.

"What's in this lot, Jes?" asked Snotty.

"Bit of Mars bar, touch of curry-flavoured crisps, hint of French fries, dawb of Big Mac, just a squish of HP tomato sauce, nothing exotic this time, Snotty."

Jessie, Bessie and Sluke took turns on Saturday morning, going down into the basement where Snotty had installed his large, state-of-the-art ice-cream-making machine which he had acquired through a mail-order advert. He had bought this, not hired it, because he was sure his mother would be very pleased by this addition to the house. Most of his acquisitions, such as the games

and music machines, were hired, just in case his mother should not deem them essential to their domestic well-being, if and when she returned.

Every Saturday one of the girls or Sluke made a fresh load of ice-cream, producing seven new and exciting varieties so that Snotty could work his way through them each morning, just to top him up, get him off to school in a good mood. The following Saturday all four of them finished off anything still left, before making a new load.

Snotty was the Supervisor, Officer-in-charge of Ice-cream, and he therefore did not do any of the hard work. He'd dreamed up the project, bought the machine, and he ordered the milk, eggs and double cream which the milkman delivered every Saturday morning. Normally Snotty hated milk, and had cancelled it after his mother left, till he saw the advert for the new wonder ice-cream-making machine.

"Well, that's the end of this lot," said Sluke, scraping his empty dish then licking it. "Could be the last lot for ever."

"I'll think of something," said Snotty.

"He won't leave this week's stuff, if you don't pay him," said Jessie.

"You can't pay him by VISA," said Bessie. "My mum tried that. Cash or cheque only."

"I've told you, I'll think of something. Don't panic."

There was a loud knocking at the front door. Snotty was the first to jump up – going straight behind the fridge to hide. He had been trying to be offhand and not worried about the problem of paying the milkman, but he was far more concerned than the other three. It wasn't the thought of the ice-cream making coming to an end but what the milkman might do about the unpaid bill. Would he report Snotty to the Social Services, or the police?

"I'm not in," whispered Snotty. "Tell him I'm not in."

"You don't even know who it is yet, you dum dum," said Sluke.

"Why should you presume it's a he anyway?" said Jessie. "Typical male assumptions."

"Go and see who it is, will you," said Snotty. "It stinks behind this fridge."

"I'll go and find out," said Bessie, getting up and going down to the basement. Carefully she looked up and on the steps she could clearly see the squat figure of Mrs Cheatham.

"No problem," said Bessie, coming back. "It's old Ma Cheatham. What should we do?"

"Just ignore her," said Snotty, stepping out from behind the fridge.

There was a deep rumbling noise. They all looked round the room, trying to work out where it had come from.

"She's breaking the door down!" said Snotty. "Call the police! No, no, hold on, *don't* call the police!"

"That was you, Sluke, wasn't it?" said Bessie, pointing at Sluke's stomach.

"I can't help it," said Sluke. "Inanition. You lot got most of the ice-cream."

"Liar, you had most," said Jessie.

"Not my fault anyway," said Sluke. "Those stupid crisps. You shouldn't have used curry flavour. They always upset my tum. In fact my mum thinks I could be getting an ulcer. You can, you know, even young people can get ulcers. I think it's stress, pressure of modern life, too much school, if you ask me . . ."

"Oh, shurrup, you old moan," said Snotty. "Your only problem is greed. We've got more important problems to worry about. How we gonna pay that stupid milkman."

"Perhaps if I talked to him nicely," said Jessie. "If I explained that your mother was out for the moment, and you were ill in bed, suffering from stress, there's a lot of it around, he might take sympathy and not want his money for another week?"

"No chance," said Snotty. "He said he wanted paying today, or else."

"I could dress up as Else," said Sluke. "Or your mother."

"Go back to sleep," said Snotty.

"Perhaps you could give him something in exchange," suggested Bessie, looking round the empty room.

"He can't have the fridge," said Sluke. "I've just worked out how to use it for scoring."

"And he can't have any of the new games," said Snotty. "They're all rented."

"How about an IOU?" said Sluke.

"He's stupid, but not that stupid," said Snotty.

"Actually, he's not stupid," said Jessie. "He's got a Ph.D."

"Is that the make of his milk float?" said Sluke. "I thought it was a BMW."

"No, it means he's a doctor," said Jessie.

"Perhaps he could look at my tum," said Sluke.

"What's he doing working as a milkman," asked Snotty, "if he's a doctor?"

"Not a medical doctor," explained Jessie. "A doctor of philosophy. My mum knows all about him. He went to Sussex University, got a degree in philosophy, but can't get a job."

"I'd rather be a milkman than hang about all day being philosophical," said Snotty.

"If he's so clever then," said Sluke, "perhaps he can solve the problem. Let's just tell him the truth. Explain what's happened. See if he can work out a way of helping us."

"Clever people still want their money," said Jessie.

There was the sound of more loud banging on the front door. Once again Bessie went down to the basement to see who it was.

"It's OK," she shouted. "It's only the postman."

Snotty looked surprised. He did not get letters, never had done, for the simple reason that he never wrote any. The post for his mother was now drying up, apart from various magazines she subscribed to, paid for in advance. That was where Snotty had seen most of his mail-order offers.

Snotty waited for the sound of the letter box being pushed open and then the postman going away, but the banging continued.

"You'll have to go," said Jessie. "It could be a big

parcel, something really good."

"No, it's always rubbish," said Snotty.

"I didn't see him holding anything big," said Bessie. "Could it be a registered letter?"

"Perhaps from your mum?" said Sluke.

Snotty's face brightened at this suggestion. He jumped up, ran to the front door and unlocked it.

"Master Nottingham Bumstead?" said the postman, a pencil between his teeth, rummaging through bits of paper. Snotty did not normally acknowledge his real name, but he was excited by the thought of what the postman might have for him.

"Sign here," said the postman, looking down at little Snotty. "If you *can* write."

Snotty signed and was handed a registered envelope, covered with African stamps. He closed the door, fixed all the bolts, and tore open the envelope. Inside was a letter, and another envelope, containing some sort of card. First he read the letter.

Hi, Snotty, my little cabbage! Still on location, still very hush hush, now in Botswana filming in the Okavango delta. I can't spell it either! Hope all is well with you. All well here, but so secret I can't tell you nuffink else, or THE STAR will get vee cross as no one must know where he is or about his project to SAVE THE WORLD (eat this letter after burning it). I have arranged with the Bank to keep paying all standing orders and credit cards, so donta worry, my sweet. THE STAR sends you his own special ticket as enclosed. Have fun. Love from your silly old Mum . . .

Snotty raced to tell the others that his mother was safe and well.

"Heh, this is brilliant," said Jessie and Bessie when they had each read the letter.

"Where's this ticket she's on about?" said Sluke. "Let's have a look."

"It'll be for some boring film," said Snotty. "She gets a lot of these preview tickets for crappy films."

Sluke opened the other envelope. Out of it fell a card, embossed with the name and coat of arms of Tottenham Hotspur, F.C. It was a ticket for one of their private Executive Boxes, to seat eight people, the sort which includes food, refreshments, TV, waitress service, plus private parking, and other facilities.

"You lucky beggar!" said Sluke.

"No interest to you, Sluke," said Jessie. "You don't follow football, being an Arsenal supporter."

"We can come with you, can't we, Snotty?" said Bessie. "We're both Spurs fans."

"You can all come," said Snotty. "And so can another Spurs fan I know . . ."

5

There was still an hour to go before kick-off. Tottenham High Road was already crowded. Lines of away supporters were marching along the pavement on one side of the road, escorted by police, some of them on horseback. Traffic on the road itself was almost stationary as cars, buses and taxis tried to move forward inch by inch.

On the other pavement, it was mainly Spurs supporters, good-humouredly walking to the match, or standing talking, waiting for friends, watching the passing show, shouting at the Man. U. fans on the other side of the road.

"'Scuse me, folks, urgent delivery," yelled a voice from the top of a milk float, cleverly making its way through the Spurs supporters, half on and half off the pavement.

It was Sluke, self-appointed look-out, directing the driver from above, pointing out gaps in the crowds.

In the driver's seat sat the milkman with Snotty beside him, clutching his Executive Box ticket.

At the back of the float, sitting on a pile of milk crates, were Bessie and Jessie, waving to the crowds and holding up their Spurs scarves.

"Come on you Spu-urs," they shouted in unison. Those pedestrians who had been a bit annoyed to find a milk float pushing through them were amused to see Bessie and Jessie, true supporters, who had managed to get an unusual lift to the match.

"It's brilliant you inviting me along, Snotty!" said the milkman, carefully steering round a hot-dog salesman. "Never been in an Executive Box before. In fact I've never had a seat before. When I was a student, I always stood on the Shelf."

"How long you been a Spurs fan, then?" asked Snotty.

"All my life," said the milkman. "It came with my mother's milk."

"You mean your mum was a milkman?"

"Good one, Snot," smiled the milkman, swerving to avoid another hot-dog salesman.

"Even at Brighton, I used to come up to follow Spurs," he continued. "You tend to inherit the team you support. You're born with it, then you follow it, through thick and thin. Only fans are truly loyal. Players and managers will move anywhere, changing their clubs, depending on the money."

Snotty wondered if he should reveal they had an Arsenal fan on board, namely Sluke, who could be about to change his club, thanks not to the money but the thought of a flash Executive seat.

On the roof, Sluke had suddenly found himself with

34

a Spurs scarf which had appeared in his hand by accident. In the other, by intent, he was holding a hot dog, which he had managed to acquire just as they were passing the last hot-dog stand.

"Heh, Doc," shouted Sluke, banging on the roof with his Doc Marten boots. "Don't go so fast. I never got no ketchup that time. Heh, that way, over there. I can see fried onions . . ."

At the main entrance to the West Stand the crowds were thickest of all, with security guards and police making sure that people without tickets were not admitted. A lot of the crowd were simply hanging around, hoping to see the players arriving, or to spot any famous fans.

"Move it," snarled a very bossy security guard, banging on the front of the milk float, then he turned to salute one of the Spurs stars purring forward in a Jaguar, lifting the barrier to let him drive into the private car park.

"I said move it," he repeated, banging on the milk float again.

"What's he on about?" said Sluke. "We're the fastest movers in all North London. Faster than Ernie. The fastest milk float in the West. Do you remember Ernie, Doc? You're educated . . ."

Sluke started to sing, swaying in time to his own tuneless tune. He had become carried away with all the crowd excitement, and also three hot dogs and four Cokes.

"Get down off that van, son," said the policeman, coming over. "What's going on here?"

"This milk float's blocking the entrance," said the security guard. "Should be banned, if you ask me, bloomin' stupid, delivering milk round here of a Saturday afternoon."

"Actually, I am not delivering milk," said the milkman, in his best Ph.D. accent. "I happen to be delivering VIP guests."

"On your bike," said the security man.

"No, it is a milk float, your first guess was correct. Jolly well spotted."

"You think you gorra lot of bottle, don't you, clever dick," said the security man.

"Right again," said the Doc. "Skimmed or semi-skimmed, the choice is up to you."

"Oh, got a right joker here," snarled the security guard.

"Just move on, please," said the policeman. "You're holding up the traffic."

"Nottingham, be kind enough to show the officer your ticket."

Snotty got out his envelope. The policeman and the security guard both looked suspicious as Snotty carefully opened it and pulled out his Executive Box ticket. The moment they saw the card, their expressions changed.

"This way sir," said the security guard, indicating a small gate for them to walk through. "Sorry about that."

"One moment," said the Doc, holding Snotty by the arm, restraining him in his seat. "Our Executive Box ticket does include parking, if I'm not mistaken, hmm, is that not so, ah ha, my good man?"

The security guard slowly lifted the barrier and let the milk float glide through. The Doc parked it between a white Rolls Royce and a red Ferrari, telling Sluke and the girls to jump down carefully.

"Make sure you don't leave sticky fingerprints or make any scratches on my milk float. It is my best one."

All five of them strolled over to a private entrance to the Executive Boxes. At the carpeted doorway, the milkman gave a wave to the security man who had tried to stop them, beckoning him over, as if perhaps he might be about to give him a tip.

"I say, Mr Security Man! Do keep an eye on my motor during the match, there's a good chap. I don't want anyone breaking into it, or pinching any mementoes, especially that one there . . ."

Snotty was not listening. He had raced up the carpeted staircase to his Executive Box, followed by Sluke, Bessie and Jessie. They couldn't get over the size and luxury of their special box, with its kitchen, TV, video, telephone, sofas, chairs and their own waitress, waiting to bring anything they might want.

Spurs beat Manchester United 3–2, a great match, enjoyed by all, especially five people in one of the best Executive Boxes. They ordered food and drink non-stop during the match and watched repeats of all goals on the video at half-time. After the game, the Spurs goal scorers came into their box to shake hands with them personally.

The players were a bit surprised to find that the SUPER-STAR SINGER who owned the box was not there, but they were pleased to find four such young, enthusiastic and highly knowledgeable supporters, all four clearly long-time Spurs fans, judging by their scarves, plus their terribly intelligent, long-haired older friend who said he was their personal chauffeur.

When they eventually staggered out, having eaten, drunk and celebrated in style, the milkman led the way back to his milk float. He checked to see if the memento was still intact, the one he had noticed early and had asked the security guard to keep an eye on.

The Spurs bag belonged to Snotty, who had insisted on taking it to the match. Being Snotty, he had then forgotten all about it, leaving it under the seat where he had been sitting beside the driver. It was not there. Someone had fixed it outside the milk float, hanging it from a strut. Doc milkman left it blowing in the triumphal breeze as they drove home. He said he had enjoyed the afternoon so much that Snotty need not pay his milk bill for the next month.

When they got to Snotty's house, Snotty invited them all in for ice-cream. Including the milkman.

2

Doctor Snotty

Sluke was first up on Monday morning. He had spent the weekend at Snotty's, with his mother's permission, and had risen early to prepare a little treat for Snotty – ice-cream in bed.

Sluke's mother had told him to be as helpful as possible, to act like a good guest or he wouldn't get invited again, to do what Mrs Bumstead told him, go to bed when she said and try to help in the house. She hadn't actually spoken to Mrs Bumstead herself, but she had heard her voice on the answering machine. Mrs Bumstead sounded as cheerful as ever, saying she would be back soon.

This was an old tape made by Snotty's mother months ago. Snotty had followed it up by ringing Sluke's mother himself, pretending to talk to his own mother in the background, saying, "Yes, Mum, OK, Mum, I'll tell her you really do want Sluke to come for the weekend, because he's your favourite guest!"

Sluke went downstairs and decided to give himself a

little treat first, as he was a bit tired, having been ever so helpful all weekend, especially to himself. This time he helped himself to two double helpings of ice-cream.

While he stood in his underpants eating his ice-cream, his tummy gave a little rumble, but it didn't worry him very much. Then his underpants began to feel a bit tight. That didn't really worry him either. He had been guzzling a lot over the weekend.

He had slept in his underpants, even though his mother had sent him with his pyjamas, freshly washed. Snotty had sniggered when he saw them. Since his mother had been away, Snotty never used such soppy things as pyjamas, preferring to sleep in his clothes. He worked out that it would save the human race months and months of their lives, if only people didn't waste time getting undressed every night.

"Where you been, fatso?" said Snotty as Sluke came back into Snotty's bedroom, carrying the ice-cream. Snotty was in his bed, surrounded by toys and games plus emergency chocolate and crisps in case of night-time starvation.

Sluke's bed was a mattress on the floor, an island in a sea of chocolate wrappers and crisp packets, signs of the emergencies they had both had to contend with over the weekend.

"Doing things for you," said Sluke. "As always."

Sluke appeared tall and thin when dressed, but now Snotty could see he was getting a slight tum. Snotty enjoyed getting at him for his eating habits, making Sluke furious, because he hated the idea of being fat.

"Before you start stuffing yourself once again," said Snotty, "I need some comics. OK. Chop chop. You know where they are."

Sluke groaned but went downstairs to the games floor. He didn't mind the odd errand – it was little enough to pay for the privilege of staying at Snotty's, though he knew that Snotty liked having him there. During the night Snotty had confessed that he sometimes did get a bit scared, sleeping in this big house all on his own.

Sluke went into the bathroom, avoiding the hole in the floor which they would have to get mended before Snotty's mum came back, *if* she ever came back. He opened the glass door of the shower which was stacked from floor to ceiling with Snotty's comics, including *Dandy*s and *Beano*s he'd first read when he was seven years old. Snotty almost preferred old comics to new

ones, knowing in advance the bits where he was going to laugh.

Sluke gathered up enough comics for both of them, and went back to Snotty's bedroom.

"Ah, this is the life!" said Sluke, dropping on to his mattress again. He flicked through the comics while licking several empty chocolate wrappers, just in case there were any scraps hiding inside, any gungy bits still lurking. Then he inspected the empty crisp packets, putting his tongue inside each one to suction up any scrinchy, inchy bits.

The phone rang on the floor below. Sluke had his head inside the last crisp packet, but he dragged himself out of it and headed for the bedroom door, wanting to save Snotty the bother of getting up.

"Don't answer it!" said Snotty. "I've left the answering machine on. No one rings me at this time of morning."

"What time is it, anyway?" said Sluke, looking for his watch amidst the mountain of wrappers and empty ice-cream plates. "Oh, no. Eight o'clock. We're gonna be late for school. Come on, Snot, move your bum."

"Move yours," said Snotty, "if you can . . ."

It didn't take Snotty long to get up. He was already in his clothes and as for washing his face or cleaning his teeth, he had given that up long ago, though he had managed a quick once-over before going to the Spurs Executive Box. Bessie and Jessie had forced him to, saying that he was beginning to pong.

Sluke took much longer. He was having trouble with his jeans, trying to fasten them behind a jukebox, so that Snotty wouldn't see him and jeer.

As they came down the stairs, they could hear someone at the front door. They stopped, listened, waited. Through the letter box came two envelopes, both addressed to Zoe Bumstead, Snotty's mother. Snotty picked them up and examined them.

"You can't open them," said Sluke. "They're for your mum."

"She said I could," said Snotty. "She said I was in charge of everything. I'm in loco thingy, that thingy Miss Eager was telling us about."

"Loco parentis?" asked Sluke.

"Sounds like it," said Snotty.

"I think that stands for loco meaning lunatic," said Sluke. "So that's about right . . ."

But Snotty was not listening to Sluke any more, so he missed this joke at his expense.

"Brilliant news," said Snotty, tearing open one of the letters. "My mum's new bank card has arrived. It'll last for the whole of next year."

For a moment he looked slightly worried. The thought of his mother being away for as long as that had not struck him before. In the night time, on his own, he told himself she would be back soon, perhaps in a week or so.

"Excellent," said Sluke.

"Now for the bad news," said Snotty, reading the other letter. "Mrs Potter wants to see my mum. She wants her to ring and make an appointment."

"Not so excellent," said Sluke. "But don't worry. We can put her off. You can say she's got a cold."

"Yeh, but I know Mrs Potter. Never trusted her. She's after me. She'll keep asking, saying she's got to see my mum. Then what do we do?"

"Has she ever seen your mum?"

"No, when I went for my interview, we saw Mr Jones, the Deputy Head."

"Then I could go as your mum," said Sluke. "She'll never know."

"Don't be stupid, you fat idiot," said Snotty. "You couldn't fool anyone."

"'Course I could," said Sluke, dancing around the hall, putting on a squeaky voice, pretending to be Snotty's mum. As he danced, he banged against the inside of the letter box, a very big letter box, the biggest in the street, which Snotty's mum had had enlarged especially to take all the books and film scripts which were sent to her for her work.

Through this large letter box came a very large arm covered in tattoos, which grabbed hold of Sluke.

"Ouch, stop it, leggo!" shouted Sluke.

"Open this door, Lucas!" said a very angry male voice.

Sluke managed to unlock the door, while still being

held by the tattooed arm.

When the door opened the owner of the arm, who happened to be Sluke's father, picked him up bodily, carried him down the front steps and threw him into the front passenger seat of a large articulated lorry, which had been left with its engine running.

"Thanks for the weekend, Snotty," yelled Sluke as the lorry drove away.

Then he was gone.

2

Snotty was not allowed out at lunch time, not even to the school cafeteria. He sat in his form room by himself; he was supposed to be writing out some extra history work Miss Eager had given him. At least she hadn't reported him to Mrs Potter.

" 'Snot fair," said Snotty, staring out of the window. He'd been staring for most of the time so far and had not yet started his work. "I was only ten minutes late. What's ten minutes when you have to spend thousands and thousands of minutes at school? I bet I've done a million minutes already.

"Let me see. Let's say six hours a day in school from the age of five, that's three hundred and sixty minutes a day five days a week, oh, and nursery school, now when did I start nursery school . . ."

"That's good, Nottingham," said Miss Eager, coming through the class-room door. "Glad to see you are properly occupied for once."

She'd had her lunch and had come back to do some marking at her own desk.

"Heh, I thought I told you to redo your history," she said, looking at his book.

"Maths," said Snotty. "I'm doing Maths. Just trying to get ahead with this new calculating and stuff."

"Then don't. I told you I want your history written up neatly before the bell goes, or you'll be in detention all week."

Snotty began copying out his history, very slowly, till he noticed Sluke's face pressed up against a window behind Miss Eager's desk, making faces at him.

Sluke had arrived just in time for school, thanks to his father taking him in his lorry, though why his father had suddenly come for him was still not clear to Snotty.

Sluke pulled up his shirt and pointed at his stomach, indicating what a big school dinner he'd had, seconds of everything, yum yum. Snotty could see funny red marks all round Sluke's waist. Probably where he'd spilt his jam roly-poly. Sluke was a messy eater.

Sluke was now pretending to be sick, writhing in agony, then pointing at Miss Eager's head, as if he was being sick all over her. Snotty tried hard not to laugh; he knew Miss Eager would give him another detention if he did.

"I think someone wants you, Miss," said Snotty, hoping Miss Eager would turn round and catch Sluke.

"Just get on with your work!" she said, without looking up.

Behind Sluke, Snotty saw Mr Jones creeping up on him. For the second time that day a large hand took

48

hold of Sluke, lifted him off the ground and carried him away.

3

"So why did your dad come for you this morning?" asked Snotty as he and Sluke walked home after school. They were late out. Sluke had got himself a detention from Mr Jones and Snotty had nobly waited for him.

"He didn't believe I was at your house," said Sluke. "He'd come to check."

"Where could you have been?" asked Snotty. "Spending the weekend at Buckingham Palace with the Queen, or at Ten Downing Street with wazzisname?"

Snotty was very good on football teams, points gained, goals for and against, position in league, best players, best reserve players, but he was not so up-to-date when it came to politics and politicians.

"My dad says I can't stay with you again," said Sluke.

"What?" exclaimed Snotty.

"He says my mum was worried about me all weekend."

"That's stupid," said Snotty. "He saw you were with me. He knows you stayed at my house. What's the problem?"

"He thinks there's something funny going on."

"He's been looking in the mirror, has he?"

"That's not funny," said Sluke. "You leave my father alone."

Sluke's father was rather hefty and overweight, with sitting in his lorry all day, driving up and down the motorways. Sluke did not like attention drawn to his father's weight, preferring to boast about his father's strength.

49

"So what's your mother worried about then?" asked Snotty.

"Dunno," said Sluke.

"I know," said Snotty. "I bet you been moaning to her about your stupid stomach, ain'tcha?"

"Well I do think I might have an ulcer growing.'

"Don't be stupid," said Snotty. "You just put it on."

"She keeps on asking me what I eat at your house, what sort of diet, is your mum a veggie, does she eat raw lentils, or seaweed, dunno why."

"Well, tell her the truth," said Snotty. "We just eat normal things. Ice-cream and sweets, crisps and Mars bars, stuff like that. You can tell her I sometimes take you out for hamburgers and chips, pizzas and things, all dead normal stuff . . . no hang on, don't say I take you out. She'll wonder where we get the money from."

When they arrived at Sluke's block of flats, they pressed the lift button for the fourteenth floor. As usual, the lift took a long time to come and when it did, out stepped Mrs Mudd, Sluke's mother.

"I was just coming to look for you," she said. "Why are you so late, Lucas?"

"Late? I'm not late."

Mrs Mudd looked at Snotty suspiciously; she thought he was a thoroughly bad influence on her beloved son.

"Miss Eager wanted us to help with the school play," said Snotty. "She's making the sets. It opens on Friday."

"Well, you're not helping on it any more, Lucas," said Mrs Mudd. "I'm taking you for an X-ray at the Royal Free on Friday. I'm worried sick about that stomach of yours."

"Oh, Mum, it's nothing, Mum," said Lucas.

"That's what you say now, but every time you've been at Snotty's, it's moan moan moan. What have you been eating there?"

"Food," said Snotty. "Just food."

"I've been trying to ring your mum all day, but all I get is that answer phone. Tell her I'm coming round this evening to see her. About nine o'clock. I'm going to get to the bottom of all this . . ."

"She's away," said Snotty quickly.

"But she was there at the weekend," said Mrs Mudd. "Wasn't she?"

"Oh, yeh, it was just this morning. She had to rush off, to Africa I think, dunno really, but just for the day really."

"To Africa, for the day? What *is* going on?"

"Dunno. Never been to Africa. Supposed to be hot, lot of animals and that . . ."

"I mean in your house. What on earth's happening there? Lucas can't keep away from it."

"Nothing," said Snotty.

"That's what you say," said Mrs Mudd. "Well, *you*'ll be in this evening, won't you?"

"Er, yes," said Snotty, hesitantly, wondering what was coming.

"Then that'll do for a start. I'll just have a look around, even if your mum hasn't come back from her day trip to Africa," she said nastily.

"Er, what is it you want to see?" asked Snotty.

"Your kitchen," she said. "That will do for a start. Come along, Lucas. I want you inside, at once!"

With that, she marched Lucas into the lift, which shot away to the fourteenth floor.

4

Snotty had tried to have a game of indoor football with Jessie and Bessie, but they'd given up. He couldn't concentrate, worrying about Mrs Mudd's arrival in just an hour's time.

Playing with only three people didn't work anyway, now that Sluke was grounded. They'd tried one against two, and the one player always got hammered. One against one had led to quite good games, with the winner playing the other one, but that had caused arguments. Snotty wanted to play in every game, even when he was beaten. It was his pitch, his ball, his rules.

For this evening, the rules had been changed slightly. Hitting the fridge, from any angle, had been banned. Jessie had cleaned it up, inside and behind, in readiness for Mrs Mudd's inspection. The sink had been unboarded and washed down.

"Do you think we should bring the cooker in?" asked Bessie. 'Make it look like a real kitchen?"

"Can't be bothered," said Snotty.

The cooker had been dragged into the back garden in the first stages of Snotty's conversion of the ground floor into a football pitch. It was now looking decidedly dirty.

"What about bringing some of the old kitchen stuff up from the basement?" said Jessie.

"Boring, boring," said Snotty.

"Just to make it look more like, you know, a kitchen?" suggested Jessie.

"This *is* our kitchen," said Snotty. "We prepare our meals here."

"How?" asked Bessie.

"We open the fridge, open our mouths, and prepare to eat. Anything else you want to know?" said Snotty.

"But you don't actually do any cooking in this kitchen," said Jessie. "Anyone can see that."

"Oh, stop wittering on," said Snotty. "OK then, if it makes you happy, we'll call this the dining room."

"Then she'll want to see the kitchen," said Bessie.

"You two are driving me potty," sighed Snotty. "Look, I'll say the kitchen is locked up. My mum always locks up the kitchen when she goes out. Keeps the mice in, ha ha."

"If you make that sort of joke, she *will* get worried," said Bessie.

"All we have to do is show her the fridge, right," said Snotty. "Just show her how amazingly clean it is, OK?

That's all she's worried about. She thinks we're poisoning her precious Lucas, giving him food that's gone off. Nothing goes off in this house. It's straight down Sluke's gob before it can go off, or go anywhere. Now just shurrup, you two, eh. Can't you see I'm reading?"

"So that's why your lips are moving," said Jessie.

Snotty was reading some of the magazines which had come for his mother over the last few weeks. They had been left lying all over the place, but this evening Jessie had gathered them into a neat pile, trying to tidy up.

Snotty flicked through a copy of *Private Eye*, saying it was childish, then *Variety*, maintaining it was in a foreign language, and then *The Stage*, reading all the adverts for auditions, hoping to find something that might suit him.

"Think I'll be a famous actor when I grow up," said Snotty. He paused, looking mournful. "*If* I grow up."

"What's to stop you?" asked Bessie.

"I'll probably get put in prison or shoved in a home, and just wither away."

54

"Now you're being pathetic," said Jessie.

"I'm not. If the Social Services find out about me living here on my own, they could do anything."

"But they won't find out."

"Oh, yeh? Mrs Mudd will probably report me right away, once she's seen this place."

"We won't let her in," said Jessie. "We can all hide and pretend no one's at home."

"She'll only come back tomorrow with Mr Mudd. You've seen the size of him. He'll push the door in. Big fat lump. No wonder Sluke is scared he'll end up like him."

"You shouldn't make comments like that," said Jessie. "People can't help their size. You're being sizeist."

"People make comments about my size all the time," said Snotty. "But then they're all stupid."

"You shouldn't call people stupid either," said Jessie.

"Oh, shurrup, stupid," said Snotty, throwing a magazine at Jessie.

"Well, if you *are* going to let her in," said Bessie, "I'd better tidy upstairs as well. She'll want to poke around everywhere."

Snotty returned to reading *The Stage*. Jessie was turning over the pages of *Private Eye*.

"Graduate, twenty-three, six feet high, strong, hardworking, adaptable, seeks challenging work," said Jessie, reading out one of the adverts. "Anything legal considered, the more bizarre the better. Own car."

"What's bizarre mean?" asked Snotty. "Does he want to work in a shop?"

"No, he wants something unusual," said Jessie. "Perhaps you should hire him as your bodyguard, to stop people like Mr Mudd getting in. You could do with a strong man about the house."

"It's a mum I want," said Snotty. 'Not a man."

Bessie returned, holding a bundle of clothes, dirty dishes, comics and bits of toys she had found lying around.

"Where should I put these, Snotty?" she asked.

"Don't care," said Snotty, rudely.

"Are these your pyjamas?" said Bessie.

"No, they're Sluke's," said Snotty, looking up. "He's forgotten them, the dum dum. Straight in the dustbin. He's not my best friend any more."

"They look a bit small for Sluke," said Bessie, throwing them at Snotty, catching him on the head. "Sure they're not yours, Snotty? Or do you still wear a Babygro . . ."

"See, that's just typical of the stupid sizeist comments I have to put up with," said Snotty.

"It was only a little comment," said Jessie.

"Yeh, they are small," said Snotty, examining the pyjamas. "The waist is two inches smaller than me. Yet he's twice my size. And weight. They must be killing him."

"How stupid," said Bessie.

"His jeans are too tight for him as well," continued Snotty. "I saw him struggling into them this morning. No wonder he's got a red mark round his middle. You should see the size of his belly."

"But he's always boasting how thin he is," said Jessie. "Saying he's never going to be fat like his dad. It doesn't make sense."

"Oh, yes, it does," shouted Snotty, jumping up, throwing his magazine on the floor. "I think it could explain everything . . ."

5

Snotty was sitting at his mother's word processor, staring at the blank screen. He'd found a disc with some space on it and had pressed C for Create. He was holding his hand to his head, looking very Creative.

Bessie was wrapping the pyjamas up neatly, using some pretty wrapping paper she had found in Snotty's mother's desk. Jessie was looking along Snotty's mother's shelves for a dictionary.

"Dear Mrs Mudd," wrote Snotty. "I just gorrin in from being in Africa tonite and my house is very excellent and imakulate and my son Snotty I mean Nottingham has been a very good boy and I am sorry to hear your Sluke has been poorly cos on accont of his stumake which I fink personally is a load of kodswallop. Is his stoopid pantz, if you arks me, yours and oblige, Mrs Bumstead (Mrs) . . ."

Snotty stood up to get some of his mother's headed notepaper, ready to put it into the printer, but Jessie pushed him back into his seat.

"That's rubbish," she said. "That won't do at all. You can't even spell the simplest word."

"W-O-R-D," said Snotty. "Anyway, you don't have to, clever clogs. It's got a Spellcheck, see. You just press this, and it gives you the right spelling. I was gonna do it later, if you hadn't been so bossy, after I'd finished Creating, after I'd let it all flow."

"Oh, yeh," said Jessie, pushing him off the seat. "You know you're the worst in the class at English. I'll do it."

Jessie deleted Snotty's letter and started again.

Dear Mrs Mudd,

she began to type.

"Copycat," said Snotty. "I done that."

"You did that,' said Bessie.

Jessie continued the letter.

I am returning Lucas's pyjamas with Nottingham, he left them over the weekend. I hope he is feeling better.

I think I know the cause of Lucas's stomach cramps. He is wearing underpants and jeans

WHICH ARE FAR TOO TIGHT FOR HIM. I KNOW HOW
BOYS GET THESE THINGS INTO THEIR HEAD, INSIST-
ING ON CERTAIN ITEMS OF CLOTHING WHICH ARE
FAR TOO SMALL FOR THEM, ESPECIALLY WHEN
THEY HAVE A TENDENCY TO OVEREAT. THEY WANT
TO PRETEND THEY ARE THINNER THAN THEY ARE.
IT IS A COMMON PSYCHOLOGICAL PROBLEM. RED
MARKS ON THE ABDOMEN ARE THE USUAL SIGNS TO
LOOK FOR. THERE IS A LOT OF IT AROUND . . .

Jessie stopped typing and told Bessie to look up the
hard spellings for her. Then she asked her to see if she
could find a medical dictionary on Snotty's mother's
bookshelves, hoping she might be able to throw in some
technical terms. All Bessie could find was a Hip and
Thigh Diet. So Jessie continued:

I SUGGEST YOU BUY LUCAS LARGER SIZES AT ONCE,
IN BOTH TROUSERS AND UNDERGARMENTS. I ALSO
SUGGEST YOU CUT OUT THE OLD LABELS AND PUT
THEM ON THE NEW CLOTHES, SO THAT HE STILL
THINKS HE IS WEARING THE SMALL SIZE! I AM SURE
IN A FEW DAYS HIS STOMACH PAINS WILL GO.

I AM WORKING ON AN IMPORTANT FILM PROJECT
THIS EVENING, SO I'D BE GRATEFUL IF YOU COULD
COME ROUND ANOTHER TIME. IF YOU DON'T MIND.
YOURS, ZOE.

Jessie read it through, checked the spelling of "grateful" in her dictionary, and then printed it out.

"Heh, that's brilliant, Jessie!" said Bessie.

"Not bad," said Snotty, grudgingly. "But it was all my idea, don't forget. I sussed out Sluke's problem."

"Right, you take it round at once, with the parcel," said Jessie. "She won't have left yet. We've still got an hour. Make sure you give it to her, not Sluke. She'll be so pleased when Sluke's better, she won't worry any more about what's happening in your house."

"I hope so," said Snotty.

"Hold on," said Jessie, as Snotty ran to the front door. "Make yourself look presentable."

Bessie and Jessie grabbed Snotty and dragged him to the sink. They washed his face under the tap, wet his hair and then combed it with their fingers, as neatly as they could.

"There, that looks as if you do have a mum at home," said Jessie.

"Off you go, my little man," said Bessie.

6

Mrs Mudd was just coming out of her flat as Snotty arrived. She didn't recognize him at first. He looked so clean and fresh, and he had a helpful smile on his face.

"Yes?" she said, suspiciously, then she answered her own rhetorical question. "No."

"Excuse me?" said Snotty, ever so hesitant.

"No, you can't play with Lucas. He's not going out. Certainly not to your house."

"My mum sent me with this note," said Snotty politely.

Jessie had even typed out Mrs Mudd's address on the envelope, so it did look very professional. After all, Snotty's mother was a professional woman, as Mrs Mudd knew.

She opened the envelope slowly, then began tut-tutting, clicking her teeth, then nodding her head.

"Lucas!" she shouted. "Come here at once!"

Sluke appeared in the hallway behind his mother, giving Snotty an apologetic smile. She grabbed his wrist with one arm and pulled up his T-shirt with the other, revealing a very fat belly, and some distinct red marks round his waist.

"This could explain everything," she said.

"Yeh, that's what my mother finks," said Snotty.

"She wasn't medically trained, was she?" asked Mrs Mudd.

"She was nearly a Doctor," said Snotty. "Of Philosophy. If she'd passed some more exams, she would have been, the ones set by the Milk Board . . ."

"What on earth are you talking about?" said Mrs Mudd. "Anyway, thank her for her help. I'm sure it will do the trick."

Mrs Mudd closed the door, still holding Sluke by his wrist. As Snotty waited for the lift, he could hear Mrs Mudd telling Sluke she was certainly not buying him new jeans, not at the moment, but he was going on a diet immediately.

3

HRH Snotty

I

It was celebration time at Marine Ices, Snotty's favourite eating place. The restaurant was crowded at Saturday lunch time, but Snotty had booked a table, best one,
in a corner, and he, Bessie, Jessie and Sluke had gone
through the menu.

A very posh family at the next table, the children in
their best clothes, were talking about the Royal Free
Hospital, about some event they were going to that afternoon.

"I was quite looking forward to having my X-ray done there," said Sluke loudly, finishing his Spaghetti Bolognese, his third round of garlic bread and his fourth Coke. "Not often they get such fine physical specimens to examine."

Sluke pulled up his T-shirt to expose his ample and unmarked tummy. At the same time, he gave a loud belch. "Pardon, I'm sure," he said.

The posh children at the next table giggled, but their parents told them to eat up their salad and not to stare at silly boys.

Sluke had made a miraculous recovery and there had been no need for him to go to hospital after all. He was slightly disappointed, as he'd planned to have a whole day off school for his X-ray, if not most of next week, but he was very pleased his pains had disappeared completely.

His mother had rung Snotty's mother, full of praise, leaving a message of thanks on the answering machine, saying she was sorry she'd been worried about Lucas staying at Snotty's house. He could now play at Snotty's any time, if of course he was invited.

This morning a large bouquet of flowers had arrived for Snotty's mother, with a note, heaping on more thanks. Luckily, Snotty had been at home to take it in.

"Knickerbocker Glories all round," announced Snotty. "We're so pleased that dear Lucas has made such a sudden recovery."

"It was amazing," said Sluke. "I just woke up yesterday and the pains had gone. I dunno why."

"Perhaps you just imagined it in the first place," said Jessie.

"I didn't," said Sluke. "It was agony. And you lot never believed me."

"It was eating too much," said Bessie. "You'd got too fat, that was all."

"I'm not fat," said Sluke. "My mum's bought me new jeans, but they're the same size as the old pair, so you're sussed."

The other three looked at each other, but said nothing.

"I've got a present for you," said Snotty, handing over a cassette tape. "It's to mark your wonderful recovery. Listen to it in the privacy of your own bedroom. Don't let your mum hear."

"Is it Heavy Metal, head-banging stuff?" asked Sluke. "Raving, rapping, housing, mousing, over the top mega, spega music?"

"No, it's your mum talking," said Snotty.

"Your what?"

"It could catch on," said Snotty. "In fact it might make Number One in the charts, when I've done a bit more work on it."

Snotty had made a copy of Mrs Mudd's voice on the tape, then he had added some backing music, plus the noise of animals eating and the sound of Spurs supporters cheering. He'd then mixed them all together on his new recording equipment, hired on his mother's VISA card.

"I had to do something all week, didn't I," said Snotty. "I got fed up playing football on my own."

Snotty paid the bill, in cash, having been to the cash point. On the way out he ordered monster double cones for everyone, flavours of their choice, so they could have something to walk with, just in case pangs of hunger overcame them on the way back to Snotty's. Once there, of course, they would get started on their own home-made ice-cream. It was Jessie's turn this week.

"I think I'll use real fruit," said Jessie. "None of that

spicy stuff we had last week."

They stopped at the fruit stalls in Inverness Street where Jessie chose the best strawberries, melons, peaches, lychees, and several exotic fruits she didn't know the names of.

"Who says we don't have a healthy diet," said Snotty, helping himself to Jessie's baskets of fruit. "Just you tell your mum what we had today, Sluke."

After the fruit stalls Snotty wandered round the tape and record stalls which covered most of the pavements on the High Street, as they do most Saturday mornings, and bought some African music.

Bessie and Jessie then led the way over the road towards the clothes market. "You need some new stuff for school," said Bessie. "I think that's why Mrs Potter wants to see your mum. She thinks you look neglected."

"Oh, don't mention her!" said Snotty. "She's written another letter to my mum, wanting to see her."

"Heh, this looks good," said Jessie, taking Snotty by the arm. "Just your size."

"I'm not buying any of that rubbish."

"OK, we will," said Jessie. She took the money out of Snotty's pocket while the other two held him tight. "Your mum expects you to look after yourself as well as the house. You've worn those same jeans for weeks, and slept in them by the look of it."

66

All three of them eventually got Snotty into a new pair of jeans, a proper shirt and a pullover. They then bought him two T-shirts.

By the time they arrived in Snotty's street they were all staggering under the weight of the shopping they had acquired, and feeling the effect of all the food, fruit and ice-cream they had consumed.

It was only when they got to the top of the steps leading to Snotty's front door, that they noticed something strange. The front door was already open.

2

"What do you think's happened?" said Sluke.

He was hiding in a gateway ten doors away from Snotty's house. Beside him was Snotty, crouching behind their piles of shopping. Jessie and Bessie were somewhere down the road on the other side of Snotty's house, pretending to play a jumping game, but carefully keeping an eye out for anyone or anything that might emerge from Snotty's front door.

They had all fled, the moment they saw the open door, scattering like magnetic iron filings. Now they were trying to work out what was going on.

"I bet you left it open," said Sluke.

"Don't be stupid. 'Course I didn't."

"Then it must be burglars," said Sluke.

"Oh, no," said Snotty. "They'll have taken my new recording stuff. It's all hired as well. What am I going to do?"

"Good job the fridge was empty," said Sluke. "Means they won't have stolen any food."

"Oh, shut up about stupid food! That's all you think about."

"Oh, no," said Sluke, peering out from the gateway. "I think the milkman's stuff's been nicked."

"You what?" said Snotty, still crouching, too small anyway to see over the gate.

"Your milkman leaves his stuff on the top step, doesn't he? Every Saturday morning. No sign of it. This is getting really serious. You'll have to call the police . . ."

"I can't," said Snotty. "They'll find out I'm living here alone."

"I wonder if the burglars are still inside," said Sluke, getting a bit bolder and stepping out of the gateway on to the pavement.

"You go and look," said Snotty. "You're bigger than me. I'll keep guard here."

"Actually," said Sluke, coming back into the gateway, "I'll have to get home. My mum expects me for lunch . . ."

"Will you shurrup about food," snarled Snotty, giving Sluke a push.

Above them, the front door of the house opened and

large dog came bounding out, heading not for Sluke or Snotty but for their piles of shopping.

"Here, what are you two doing, messing about on my step?" said an angry-looking man, coming down the steps after the dog.

"Sorry, just resting," said Snotty, getting up. "Been doing some shopping for my mum."

"Oh, it's you, is it," said the man. "Ain't seen your mum recently. How is she?"

"Fine, fine," said Snotty, gathering up the shopping bags and pushing Sluke ahead.

"Well, you'd better hurry home with the shopping," said the man. "Your mum will be waiting for you."

Sluke and Snotty picked up their bags and walked towards Snotty's house, watched by the man. Outside Snotty's front door, they stopped, scared to go any further.

"Heh, I've just thought of something," said Sluke. "Perhaps your mum *is* at home. She's come back, while we've been out shopping . . ."

For a moment, Snotty's face lit up, then he shook his head. "She wouldn't leave the front door open. And her car's not back."

While they waited, neither of them daring to go up Snotty's front steps in case any burglars should rush out, Bessie and Jessie appeared from the other side of the street. They rushed right past the hesitant, cringing figures of Sluke and Snotty, bounded up the steps and through the open front door.

"Cor, they're brave," said Sluke.

Snotty and Sluke listened, then carefully they crept up the steps and peeped into the front hall.

Down the stairs came old Mrs Cheatham, followed by Bessie and Jessie, both smiling.

"How did you know it was her?" asked Sluke.

"We saw her through your top window," explained Jessie. "So we knew it was all right."

"It's not all right," said Mrs Cheatham. "It looks as if an earthquake has hit your house. Where's your mum?"

"Oh, she's not in, then?" said Snotty, putting on his dopey look.

"'Course she's not in," said Mrs Cheatham, resting against the hall wall, completely out of breath. She had managed to go all the way upstairs, despite her problems with her bad legs, her bad eyesight, her bad hearing.

"Are you all right, Mrs Cheatham?" asked Jessie.

"I'll manage," she said. "I'm just shocked by the state of this house. Looks like a bomb has hit. Where is your mother, anyway?"

"She'll be back soon," said Snotty.

"That's what you've been saying for weeks. Who made all this mess? Where did that hole in the bathroom come from? What's happened to your kitchen?"

"Kitchen?" said Snotty, still being dopey. "Oh, my mum's moved all the kitchen stuff downstairs in the basement, you know how she's always moving things around, changing stuff and that . . ."

"I never looked downstairs," said Mrs Cheatham, heading for the stairs, but Snotty blocked her path. Jessie and Bessie brought her a chair to sit on, saying she must be tired going up and down all those steps.

"Would you like a cup of tea?" asked Jessie.

"That would be nice, dear," said Mrs Cheatham.

"We ain't got none," said Snotty, making a face at Jessie. "My mum's given up tea. It's her new ecological diet, brought back from Africa. Save the tea forests. Tea leaves have feelings, you know. Tell you what, have some strawberries."

Snotty pulled a punnet out of a bag and handed it to Mrs Cheatham. Half the strawberries had been eaten and the rest were covered in dog's saliva.

"Ugh, you trying to poison me, or something?"

"Sorry about that," said Snotty, pulling things out of another bag. "Have a pair of jeans . . ."

Mrs Cheatham got up from the chair, pushing Snotty

71

away, and once again headed for the basement stairs.

"Shush," said Jessie, taking Mrs Cheatham's arm, putting a finger to her lips. "We're not supposed to disturb."

"Is your mother working down there, then?" asked Mrs Cheatham.

"Secret project," said Snotty. "That's why she's moved her office down there. Some big film she's on. No one must know about it."

"So she's in, is she?"

"In the pink," said Snotty.

"OK then, I won't disturb her just now," said Mrs Cheatham.

"Is that why you were upstairs, looking for her?" asked Jessie, innocently.

"I was looking for the fridge, if you must know."

"And did you find it?" asked Bessie.

"With a struggle," said Mrs Cheatham. "I've put your milk and stuff in it, so it doesn't go off, you see . . ."

"Thanks awfully, Mrs Cheatham," said Jessie, gripping her arm more firmly and ushering her to the front door, helped by Bessie.

"Tell your mum I'll come back and see her later," she said to Snotty as she went out.

"You'll be lucky," said Snotty under his breath.

3

The music was on at full blast, shaking the whole of the top floor, the music floor of Snotty's house.

Snotty was mixing in some bits of the tape of the new African music he had bought, adding it to his Mrs Mudd record. He was wearing earphones, but he still insisted that the music should be on full blast, to resonate round

the room, or his studio as he now liked to call it.

"You'll have Mrs Cheatham complaining," said Bessie.

"She won't hear," said Snotty. "She's half deaf."

"But she's not daft," said Jessie. "She'll be back soon, demanding to see your mum."

"Yeh, what we gonna do next time?" said Sluke.

"Do wa, boop booop, grug grug, wham bam, dee doom," yelled Snotty, swaying in time to the music.

"I don't think that will impress her," said Bessie.

"Turn that stuff down, Snotty," said Sluke. "I can't hear myself eat."

Sluke had brought up a large bowl of the latest batch of ice-cream hidden under a Spurs scarf so that Snotty would not realize what he'd done. The ice-cream was supposed to last Snotty all week for his breakfast, but he was too busy with his music to notice what Sluke was eating.

Bessie and Jessie were both helping Snotty with the music, contributing ideas, operating the synthesizer, playing bits on the keyboard, harmonizing and humming along. Sluke, being tone-deaf, felt rather out of it, but the ice-cream was helping to keep him occupied.

"What I don't understand," said Sluke, "is how she got in."

"Who?" asked Jessie.

"Old Ma Cheatham."

"You know how," said Jessie. "She has a key for this house. Snotty's mother gave her one, yonks ago, for use in emergencies."

"Oh, yeh," said Sluke, covering his ice-cream with the Spurs scarf, as Snotty was swaying his way, but they were all ignoring Sluke, letting him witter on while they worked on their music.

"I wonder if one of her keys is in this house," said Sluke. "I know, why don't we go into her place when she's out, have a look round. What do you think, you lot?"

"What for?" asked Jessie.

"See if there's anything worth eating."

"What a pig you are," said Jessie, throwing an empty cassette case at him.

"Heh, that nearly hit Snotty's scarf. Have you no respect?"

Sluke got up and wandered round the room looking at musical machines till they pushed him away. Then he found a radio and tried to tune in.

"Soon be time for the half-time results," said Sluke. "See how many goals Crystal Palace are hammering Spurs by, ha ha."

"Put that thing down, Sluke," said Jessie. "Can't you see we're busy?"

Sluke went to the front window and stood there looking out, humming aimlessly to himself, muttering from time to time that he was starving.

"We've got to decide what we're going to call ourselves," said Bessie.

"Snotty," said Snotty, taking off his cans for one moment, then putting them on again. "Always thought that was a nice name."

"We've helped as much as you," said Bessie. "Two girls and one boy made the music, so I think we should have a feminine name."

"What about Jes 'n Bes?" said Jessie.

"Sounds like a cowboy and his horse," said Sluke.

"Shurrup you," said Snotty.

"How about calling us Zoe, after Snotty's mum?" said Bessie. "This *is* her house."

"But we'll have to spell it in a new way," said Jessie. "How about Zo-Ee?"

"Sounds groovy," said Bessie.

"Sounds mega," said Jessie.

"Sounds stupid," said Sluke. "You should be working on a way of stopping Mrs Cheatham coming back, not messing about with this crappy music."

Jessie threw another empty cassette case at him but it missed, banging against the window. Then they went back to their music-making.

"Heh, look what I can see," said Sluke. "Coming into your street, Snotty. Amazing. Can't believe it. Your street really is coming up, Snotty."

"You can't catch us that way," said Jessie. "Go back to sleep."

"No, really, come and see," said Sluke. "There's a Rolls Royce in your street."

"So what?" said Jessie. "Cars are really boring."

"It's stopped right outside your front door, Snotty. It's enormous. And it looks as if it's got a sort of flag at the front . . ."

"Look, shurrup, Sluke, we're busy," said Snotty, ignoring Sluke and concentrating on his music. "Jessie, pass me that reel, please."

"Guess what's happened now," said Sluke a few minutes later. "Someone's coming to your front door, Snotty. In a uniform. Can't be that social worker. They don't drive Rolls Royces. Could be the secret police . . ."

From the front door there was the sound of loud knocking, clearly heard by all of them, even on the top floor.

"Not in this room," said Snotty, leading the way along the hall, past the door of the open-plan living room. He quickly closed it, hoping they had not seen inside. "There's a phone upstairs you can use."

He was being very polite and welcoming, for Snotty. When the driver of the Rolls had knocked at the front door, saying he had broken down and could he use a phone, Snotty had been suspicious at first, but then he had grudgingly allowed him to come in. The driver had been followed into the house by two ladies, both uninvited.

"An indoor football pitch," exclaimed one of his unexpected guests, who had managed to catch a glimpse of what lay inside the door Snotty had closed. "How marvellous! Just what William and Harry always wanted. Do go and get them, would you."

She turned to her companion, an equally elegant and very well-spoken lady, who went back down the hall and then returned with two young boys.

"You don't mind if they have a game, do you?" said the first lady.

"No problem," said Snotty. "You can play with them, Sluke. They look about your level."

Sluke had followed Snotty down the stairs, to see who had been knocking at the front door, leaving the girls upstairs, still making their music.

Sluke went off to play football with William and Harry, moaning that it wasn't fair, why did he have to get stuck with the kids.

Meanwhile Snotty led the way up the stairs to the first floor. He showed the driver where the phone was, apologizing for all the mess, all the toys and games. He tried to clear a bit of space where the two ladies could sit down. Several pieces of his mother's better furniture had been brought up some time ago for the visit of Mrs Pratt, the social worker, but they were now covered in comics and sweet papers.

"Sorry about this," said Snotty.

"It's frightfully good of you," said the assistant lady, staring round, clutching her handbag, as if looking for something . . .

Oh, no, thought Snotty. She's going to ask for the bathroom. Not only was it now a snooker room, but there was the matter of the hole in the floor.

"Er, I don't suppose by any chance," began the assistant lady, "that you have a . . .?"

"It's not working," said Snotty quickly.

78

"Nothing seems to be working today," sighed the assistant lady. "Our car phone isn't working, the security car got lost, then our car packed up on us."

"Jolly lucky we broke down outside your house," said the leading lady, "or we would not have had the chance to see your marvellous home. So clever, so original, wish we had something like this."

"Easy enough to do, if you've got your own house," said Snotty. "You got your own house, then?"

"Not exactly," said the leading lady. "It belongs to the family. I don't think they'd allow us to do what you've done . . ."

She wandered round, exclaiming at all the toys and games. The chauffeur was on the telephone, holding on, waiting for a mechanic to find something.

"All I was going to ask," began the assistant lady, looking round again, "is if by chance you have another phone? You see we have to contact the Palace."

"There's no score," said Snotty.

"What?" said the assistant lady.

"Nil nil, half-time. Palace have been dead jammy. Spurs missed a penalty . . ."

"You're a Spurs fan are you?" said the leading lady. "William and Harry both love Manchester United."

"So they don't follow football," said Snotty.

"That's one of their jokes as well," said the leading lady. She had now stopped in the middle of the room, listening to the music from above.

"Sounds good," she said, going to the doorway, trying to hear the music more clearly.

"Her Highness likes all music," said the assistant lady.

"Yes, she is tall," said Snotty.

"Is it African?" asked the leading lady.

"Sort of," said Snotty. "We're just working on it. Mixin' a few tracks an' that."

"You have your own recording studio? How exciting. May I go and listen?"

"Come on, then," said Snotty. "But don't touch anything."

Bessie and Jessie each had their earphones on, concentrating on the music. They did not at first hear Snotty and his two visitors entering the recording room.

"These are two of my technical people," said Snotty grandly, waving in the direction of Jessie and Bessie. "I do all the real creative work."

"What a lie," said Jessie and Bessie, turning round when they heard his voice. "It's our group as well."

"I say, what do you call yourselves?" asked the leading lady.

"Zo-Ee," said Jessie.

Jessie stared at the leading lady, Snotty's visitor whom he was now showing round the room, feeling she had seen her somewhere before. Then suddenly she put her hand to her mouth, taking a quick breath, and gave Bessie a nudge.

Snotty went over to the controls, showing off his expertise, winding back the tape to the beginning, to see what the girls had added.

"You don't mind if I listen, do you?" said the leading lady, looking for a place to sit down. The floor was very dusty. Snotty had never cleaned or Hoovered since his mother left.

"Don't sit there," shouted Jessie, just as the leading lady was about to sit down on the Spurs scarf.

"Sacred territory, is it?" she said smiling, carefully picking it up. Underneath she found Sluke's half-empty bowl of ice-cream. He had forgotten to finish it, being too busy watching the Rolls out of the window.

"Have it if you like," said Jessie. "I made it. Full of goodness. Fresh strawberries, melons and lychees."

"Yum yum," said the leading lady.

She found a relatively clean bit of rug and sat on it, listening to the music and eating her ice-cream.

Jessie offered to get the assistant lady some ice-cream, but she declined, standing at the window, watching below where the driver had now opened the bonnet of the car and was doing something with the engine.

"This is fun," said the leading lady, getting up and dancing by herself in time to the music. "Much more amusing than opening the new wing at the Royal Free Hospital."

"Ah," said the assistant lady, just as the tape finished. "He's waving at us. I think the car is fixed. We'd better be going. With a bit of luck, we'll only be ten minutes late. If you are ready, Ma'am."

For a moment, Snotty thought his mother had come back. He went cold, giving a little shiver, then he realized it was the leading lady who was being addressed. Very strange. Surely the other lady couldn't be her daughter.

"Thanks awfully for having us," said the leading lady, shaking hands with Bessie, Jessie and Snotty in turn. "Very entertaining."

The two ladies went down the stairs, followed by Snotty, Jessie and Bessie.

"William and Harry, we're orf!" shouted the leading lady.

Harry appeared at once, but there was no sign of his brother.

"William, where are you?" shouted his mother again.

Snotty went into the football pitch where Sluke was standing alone, caught in the act of changing the scores on the wall, to his advantage of course.

"Where's William?" said Snotty.

"I thought he was with you," said Sluke.

"How could he be?" said Snotty. "We left him with you."

"Stupid kid," said Sluke.

"That's no way to speak about an heir to the throne," said Jessie, coming into the room.

"Didn't notice his hair style," said Sluke. "If he'd been a skinhead, I'd have noticed that, but it was just sort of floppy . . ."

"Oh, shurrup," said Jessie. "Don't you realize you've lost the next but one King of England . . ."

5

They held a meeting in the hall, trying to keep calm and go over what had happened. Sluke at first said that William had just sort of disappeared, just walked out of the room, without saying a word, but he couldn't remember exactly when or why.

"You wanted to play one a side, didn't you?" said Jessie. "That's why you didn't notice when he sloped off, and you didn't care."

"Yeh, well, maybe," said Sluke. "But I thought he'd gone upstairs with you lot, listening to the stupid music and that."

"But he hadn't," said Jessie. "So it's all your fault. You were supposed to look after him."

"Oh, I remember now," said Sluke, "he said he wanted the toilet."

"Oh, I'm sure he would never say that," said the assistant lady indignantly.

"So did you take him to the lavvy?" asked Snotty.

"If anything, William would have asked for the loo," continued the assistant lady, giving a slight shudder.

There then started an argument about correct usage. Snotty, like his mother, always used the word lavatory, though now and again he shortened it to lavvy, which his mother did not care for. In Sluke's house, polite usage was to say toilet. Didn't everyone say toilet, asked Sluke. Royal custom, according to first-hand evidence, preferred the word loo, which is what William would have said. All of this amazed Jessie and Bessie who said they used none of those words. In their house, so they explained, they always used the word bathroom to cover all functions of – er – a bathroom nature.

"Oh, no," shrieked Jessie, "you didn't send him to the bathroom, did you?"

"I didn't send him anywhere," said Sluke. "I just said there's one under the stairs, and one upstairs, that's all I said, if I said anything, but I was busy at the time, scoring this brilliant goal . . ."

They quickly looked in the ground floor lavatory/ toilet/loo, which was under the stairs and hard for a stranger to find, as it looked like a cupboard. It was empty.

They then all rushed upstairs to the bathroom, led by Jessie and Bessie. They had been the first to realize the significance of the bathroom. This was where some weeks previously there had been a series of changes, some by intent, such as the bath being converted into a snooker table, one of Snotty's more inspired ideas, and some by accident, such as a flood which resulted in a hole in the floor. Snotty had covered it over temporarily with one of his mother's Indian rugs – and then forgotten it.

Bessie got to the bathroom first and tried the door. It was locked. She banged the handle, trying to force it open.

"Wills, are you in there?" asked his mother, getting down on the floor and trying to look underneath the door. All of them crouched beside her, looking for cracks in the door.

"William, darling, do open the door!" pleaded the assistant lady.

They all listened carefully. At first they could hear nothing, then there was the sound of a window being forced up.

"Oh, no," said Sluke. "He's trying to climb out. He'll break his bloomin' neck or split his head open . . ."

"It won't be the first time," said the assistant lady. "Remember the time he collided with a golf club."

"William, open this door at once!" said his mother firmly, giving the assistant lady a glare.

"I can't," said a faint and rather frightened voice. "It's stuck."

"Well, don't panic, darling," said his mother.

They could hear him climbing down from the window-sill on to the bathroom floor. Bessie and Jessie put their hands to their ears. If he stood on the wrong part of the Indian rug, he could be in more danger than climbing out of the window.

"It wasn't my fault," complained William plaintively. "The door stuck when I shut it."

They could hear him clearly now behind the door. He turned the handle again, but it still wouldn't open.

"I did try to shout for you," said William, "but you were all listening to some music."

"Sorry about that, darling," said his mother.

"I'll just try the window again," said William. "I got it open just now. There's a drainpipe not far away. Looks jolly easy. I'll just move this table on top of the bath so I can climb a bit higher . . ."

"A table?" exclaimed the assistant lady. "On top of a bath?"

"Ouch, urgh, nahhh . . ." yelled William. There was a loud crash.

86

"Darling, are you OK?" shouted his mother.

There was silence. Bessie and Jessie were sure that he had fallen through the hole in the floor.

"It's all right!" said William suddenly. "I just stood on a snooker ball."

"A snooker ball?" said the assistant lady. "In a bathroom?"

"Oh, stop making inane remarks," said William's mother.

"I'm now on the windowsill," announced William. "If I just lean out a bit further I'll be able to . . . ohhh!!"

"I can't bear it any more," moaned his mother. "Can't someone *do* something?"

"William, just stay on the windowsill," shouted Snotty. "Don't move any further. And don't stand on the carpet whatever you do. Sluke come with me."

Snotty raced downstairs. They got the step ladder from the basement and set it up in the middle of the football pitch. Sluke was sent up the ladder first, to tear away the bit of hardboard that had been tacked over the hole in the ceiling, not for any artistic reasons but to stop their football getting lost. Sluke then held the ladder while Snotty climbed through the hole.

William nearly fell off the windowsill when he saw the Indian carpet rising before him. He'd begun to feel dizzy anyway, at the thought of climbing down the drainpipe.

"This way, Wills," spluttered Snotty, his mouth filled with bits of dust and plaster and his head covered in Indian carpet.

He helped William through the hole and they both came down the ladder. Sluke's attention wandered just as they stepped on the bottom rung; he saw some football scores on the wall he'd forgotten to alter. Snotty, William and Sluke all fell in a heap, but fortunately none of them was hurt.

The noise brought the others rushing down the stairs. William was given a huge hug by his mother – who then proceeded to give Snotty a hug as well.

"Our hero," she said. "What would we have done without you?"

"Ugh," said Snotty, a bit embarrassed at being hugged.

William was brushed down. Snotty was thanked again, and so was Sluke, for playing football with Harry if not William.

As the visitors were walking down the front hall, Mrs Cheatham's eyes could be seen peering through the letter box. She'd watched the Rolls, observed people going inside Snotty's house, heard banging and shouting, windows opening, things crashing, and had naturally come to investigate.

The assistant lady opened the door and walked straight into Mrs Cheatham, sending her sprawling. Both ladies immediately helped Mrs Cheatham to her feet.

"I do hope you're all right," said the leading lady.

"You should be a bit more careful. Bloomin' cheek, coming out of a door without looking properly, who do you think you are anyway . . ."

Mrs Cheatham got to her feet and glared at the two ladies.

"Oh . . . er . . . oh, I don't believe it."

"I say, you are all right, aren't you?" said the leading lady.

"I'm all right, thank you, your Highness, your Majesty, your Excellency . . ."

"Are you sure?" said the leading lady.

Up and down the street neighbours were peeping out, watching the scene on Snotty's front-door step. They'd all spotted the Rolls and, like Mrs Cheatham, had wondered who Snotty's posh-looking visitors might be.

"Once again," said the leading lady, turning to shake Snotty's hand, "many thanks indeed."

Across the road there was a flash as a photograph was taken from the top flat at number 26. At number 24 they had even managed to get out their camcorder.

"It was awfully good of you to have us," said the leading lady. "Great house, brilliant ice-cream, marvellous facilities, and I did love Zo-Ee . . ."

"You've been talking to Zoe?" said Mrs Cheatham.

"Listening to her," said the leading lady. "And I'm sure it's going to be a great project. Goodbye . . ."

6

The *Letter* came second delivery. It meant that Snotty only saw it when he came home from school. It didn't have a stamp, which was the first thing that struck him as fairly peculiar. There was simply a funny red circle and an embossed seal on the back of the envelope.

"Don't just rip it open," said Sluke, coming into the house behind Snotty. "You know I collect that sort of stuff."

"I thought you collected stamps?" said Snotty. "Well, there's no stamp on this, so hard cheese."

"Let's have a look," said Sluke, trying to grab it. "Heh, that's even better! I'll have that for my postal history collection."

"What's that, then?" said Snotty.

"That means envelopes, or covers as we experts call them. It includes the study of different postal markings. This one looks official, because of the red franking. Open it carefully."

"How boring," said Snotty, ripping the envelope

open. "I bet it's from Social Services. That cruddy old Mrs Pratt, poking her nose into my business again."

Snotty's angry face began to turn into Snotty's happy face, as he slowly read the letter. Then he handed it triumphantly to Sluke.

> Kensington Palace
> London, SW1
> Dear Mrs Bumstead,
> HRH the Princess of Wales has asked me to write and thank you for the hospitality and kindness she received at your house the other day. She was particularly grateful to your charming son "Snotty", hero of the hour, for his help with Prince William. The ice-cream was also much appreciated! Good luck with the Project Zoe. We wish it all success.
> Yours sincerely,
> Lady in Waiting

"That's not fair," said Sluke, when he'd finished reading the letter. "It was me who had to play with those soppy kids. I did all the hard work. You just sat around chatting, listening to your stupid music and eating my ice-cream, which I was saving, so you owe me some. If you ask me, I should get a knighthood, for giving up my ice-cream and playing with those kids."

"It's my house, remember," said Snotty, taking the

letter back from Sluke. "*My* indoor pitch, *my* game, *my* rules which I invented."

"So? I still did all the work. OK then, I'll accept an OBE . . ."

Sluke took a drink from the fridge and sat down on the football pitch floor to study the envelope, examining the franking and the seal.

Snotty suddenly rushed up the stairs, and came down a minute later, moaning and groaning, shouting and cursing, still holding the *Letter* in his hand.

"Who's stolen all the pens in this house?" yelled Snotty, opening drawers and emptying things out.

"I dunno," said Sluke. "It's your house, remember."

"I've *got* to find a pen," shouted Snotty. "This is urgent."

Sluke stood up languidly and fetched Snotty's Spurs bag which Snotty had dumped on the hall floor after school.

"Here's a Biro," said Sluke, producing one from the bag. "You can never find things, can you, Snotty."

"That's red, you idiot!" said Snotty, snatching it from Sluke's hand and hitting him with his bag. "I want a *black* pen."

"Oh, why didn't you *say*?" said Sluke. He slowly took his best black felt-tip pen from a string round his neck.

He kept it hidden there, under his T-shirt, so that people like Snotty could not borrow it.

Snotty laid the letter flat on the hall shelf. Very carefully, he read it through again and then added one small mark – a comma between the words "Project" and "Zoe".

"What you doing that for?" said Sluke. "You're mucking it up, and it's not even your letter."

"Now read it," said Snotty. "It looks as if she's talking to my mum personally, saying 'Good luck with the Project, Zoe,' instead of wishing us good luck with our Project Zoe record."

"Yeh," said Sluke. "I suppose it does. So what?"

"So it looks as if she knows my mum. As if my mum was here when she visited us. Get it? All the nosy neighbours in our street will be convinced that my mum is here. Well, most of the time anyway. Oh, give it to me, you dum dum."

Snotty took the letter to his mother's room and made twenty copies of it on her photocopying machine.

"Take one to your mum," said Snotty. "Let her see it. Flash it around. Feel free."

"What about Jessie and Bessie?"

"Yeh, one for them as well," said Snotty. "And one for Mrs Cheatham. One for that pig with the dog. Two for the people opposite taking photographs. One for Mr Patel to put in his shop window. One for Marine Ices to frame and put on the wall with the letters from other famous people. Oh, yeh, one for the *Ham and High*. It'll probably make their front page.

"We want as many people as possible to know we've had Royal Visitors. It should give us a breathing space for a few weeks. And make us pretty famous."

4

Snotty and the Rent-a-Mum

I

Mrs Potter's ultimatum came on a Wednesday morning. It arrived by recorded delivery at Snotty's house before he went to school. At school a copy of it was put into his hand by Mrs Potter's secretary, who made him sign that he had received it. When he got home from school he turned on the answering machine to find the same message repeated. Snotty's mother was to appear at school a week on Friday at five o'clock, ten days ahead. Or else.

For a day Snotty was in a daze, unable to concentrate his normally incisive mind. Sluke dropped some of the latest flavour of ice-cream on his head, by mistake of

course – Sluke never wasted ice-cream – but Snotty didn't seem to notice.

When Jessie or Bessie mentioned the appointment, he muttered that he would go into hiding, or run away to sea on a tramp steamer (he'd always wanted to be a tramp), or go on the road with a travelling theatre.

He was flicking over the pages of his mother's copy of *The Stage* at the time. And it was this that suddenly galvanized his slumbering mind into instant and brilliant action.

"We'll hire one!" he shouted.

"Hire what?" said Sluke.

"A mum, of course," said Snotty. "This paper is full of people looking for parts. Trained people, who can act. We'll hire one of them to be my mum."

"What if she doesn't look like your mum?" said Sluke.

"That doesn't matter," said Snotty. "Mrs Potter has never seen my mum. As long as she can act like my mum might act, that'll do."

All four of them lay on the floor and spread out the pages of *The Stage*, studying the advertisements very carefully. Jessie was sent to get a sheet of clean paper and a pen, as her handwriting was the best.

They found there were two columns of classified adverts, one headed "Artists Wanted (Professional)", which seemed mainly for exotic dancers to work abroad, and the other "Artists Wanted (Amateur)" which seemed to be for people to act in local theatres or panto-mimes.

They decided to advertise in the professional column, because they would need a high standard of acting to convince Mrs Potter. But they were a bit confused by the exotic dancing.

"What's exotic dancing?" said Sluke.

"Dunno," said Snotty. "But we'd better put it in. Seems to be mentioned in most of the ads."

"OK, then," said Sluke. "Write this down, Jessie: 'Someone to be Snotty's mum and do exotic dancing . . .'"

"Don't be stupid," said Jessie. "We can judge if someone's a good mum, but how can we judge exotic dancing if we don't know what it is?"

"She's right," said Bessie. "And, anyway, Mrs Potter would get suspicious if someone starts doing exotic dancing all over her office."

Once again, they studied all the advertisements, noting that most of them gave exact details, such as age of the part to be played.

This led to further arguments. Snotty maintained his mother was twenty-seven, which was what she had always told him, but Jessie and Bessie said this must be a lie. It would mean she had had Snotty when she was about fifteen, which was ridiculous.

Then there were discussions about what his mother looked like, the colour of her hair, complexion, distinguishing marks. Snotty himself did not seem to be sure what she looked like, at least he couldn't think of the right words to describe her, but then she had been away for many weeks now. In the end Jessie produced the best solution. Applicants must send a photograph. Quickly she wrote down her advert in her best handwriting before anyone could change it:

Wanted: actress to play part of mother, aged 30–40, short season only, but excellent remuneration for the right person. Send photo and CV. Box 124X.

2

They waited all weekend, then Monday, Tuesday and
Wednesday: yet still not one response. By that time they
were all arguing among themselves, blaming each other
for getting it wrong. It meant there were only two days
to go: their last two days of freedom, perhaps for ever,
before all was discovered.

"Your fault," said Snotty. "I wanted to put in a phone
number. We'd have had lots of replies by now."

Bessie and Jessie had persuaded him that a phone
number was a bad idea. If you advertised your real
phone number, people could check up on you. Who, for
example? said Snotty. Just people, official people, any
people, wanting to know what was going on.

Their mother always used a box number when she
sold things, which meant that people sent their replies
to the newspaper who then passed them on. That way
you could study the handwriting, the address, perhaps
a photograph, before deciding if the applicant was suitable.

"If we get nobody," said Snotty, "you'll have to do
it, Sluke."

"Ha ha," said Sluke.

He often dressed up as an adult, of uncertain sex,
when helping Snotty to get money out of the cash-
dispensing machine on busy days, but that could not be
done very often, or very convincingly. After all, Mrs
Potter knew Sluke.

"How about your friend Doc milkman?" said Sluke.
"With his long hair and ear-ring, he could easy look like
a woman."

"Not like my mum, you pig," said Snotty, giving Sluke a kick.

"Actually," said Jessie, "looks are not the most important thing. It's how you behave yourself, whether you can talk and think and act like a mum. That's going to be the difficult part for any actress."

"So difficult, no one wants the job," moaned Snotty. At that moment there was a gentle knock at the front door, then another, equally hesitant.

"It must be someone after the job," said Sluke, jumping up.

"Don't be daft," said Snotty. "No one knows the address. We gave a box number."

"Perhaps she thinks this is the box," said Sluke. "You have rather knocked the house about."

"Just sit down and shurrup," said Snotty.

The knocking started again; then they could hear someone fumbling with the letter box.

"You can answer it, Sluke," said Snotty, "for giving cheek."

It was Mrs Cheatham on the front step, beaming.

"Is Snotty in?" she asked, all smiles.

"He might be," said Sluke. "Who wants him?"

"Everybody, if you ask me," said Mrs Cheatham. "He's suddenly become so famous. So I hope he can spare me just a few minutes?"

"He's in conference," said Sluke, rudely. "Tell me what you want. I'm his spokesman."

"OK, then, you'll do. As you're so big and strong. You can come and give me a hand."

She stepped over the little wall on to her front steps and through her front door, followed by Sluke. Just inside her door was an enormous grey mailbag, filled to the brim with letters.

"This came this morning when Snotty was at school," she said. "Good job I was in. Now can you manage them, Sluke? I'll just lead the way . . ."

" 'S all right," said Sluke, lifting the bag on to his thin shoulders, staggering under the load. "I can manage. Thank you very much."

He staggered across to Snotty's front steps, managing to stop Mrs Cheatham following him, though she was desperate to get in.

"What do you think the letters are for, Lucas?"

"For Snotty."

"I mean why is he getting so many?"

"Fan letters, I should think," said Sluke.

"Well, he is ever so famous, since the Royal visit," said Mrs Cheatham. "Everybody's talking about him, saying what a lovely boy he is. I always said so myself. I remember taking him out in his pram when he was little, you know, what a treasure. Sometimes I baby-sat, when his mother was out at a film première, oh, he was always . . ."

"Thank you, Mrs Cheatham," said Sluke. "Sorry you've been bothered. And goodbye."

Sluke closed the door, with Mrs Cheatham outside.

Snotty, Bessie and Jessie could not believe their eyes when Sluke emptied out the mailbag. There were 1,713 applications for the job. Most contained photographs. All contained phone numbers.

"Cor, where have they all come from?" said Sluke.

"It's because of the unemployment," said Jessie. "I think every out-of-work actress in the world has applied for the job."

They started at once sorting through the applications. Snotty said all bad handwriting had to go. Being a bad handwriter himself, he didn't want to have to read bad handwriting. Silly jokes won extra points; his mother always made silly jokes in letters. As for the photographs, Snotty had the final say on which ones looked most like his mother.

It took them two hours to make a short list of fifty. Then they started ringing people, saying auditions would be tomorrow from four o'clock onwards, could they be there, yes or no? When ten people had said yes, no question, they would be there, Snotty was bored and told the others to put the rest of the letters back in the mailbag.

"Phew," said Snotty. "I'm knackered."

"The real hard work is to come," said Jessie.

"How do you mean?" said Sluke.

"What on earth are we going to ask them?"

RENT-A-MUM: MULTIPLE CHOICE QUESTIONS FOR ALL
THOSE APPLYING TO ACT AS SNOTTY'S MUM. TICK ONE
ONLY. THANK YOU.

A. When Snotty says, "I'm bored, Mum," do you
answer:
1 Only boring people are bored.
2 Being bored is part of the growing-up process, so
the sooner you learn to live with it the better, my
lad.
3 So am I, Snotty. I know, let's go to the pictures
together.

BORED →

B. When Snotty wakes up in the morning and says he
feels sick and is not well enough for school, do you:
1 Groan, then pretend not to hear him, carrying on
reading *The Independent*.
2 Say, "It's your own stupid fault. I told you not to
go out in the rain yesterday without a jacket."
3 Say, "Poor you. Have the morning off, then if you
feel a little bit better at lunch time, we'll go to
McDonalds."

HAPPY →

C. When Snotty comes home from school and says he has not been picked for the team, do you say:

   1 I'm not surprised. You never went to training.

   2 I hope that means next time you'll try a bit harder.

   3 I think you're right, Snotty. That teacher has always been against you.

UNHAPPY

D. When Snotty says that everyone in his class has got Nintendo/ a TV in his bedroom/ his own snooker table, do you say:

   1 That doesn't mean to say you should have one.

   2 That's funny, I was talking to Jessie's/Bessie's/ Sluke's mum only yesterday and they certainly haven't got such things.

   3 Great idea, Snotty. We'll get one at once, only bigger.

BORED →

E. When Snotty says, "I've nothing to do, Mum," do you say:

   1 When I was your age, I only had old saucepans and spoons to play with, but I was always gainfully occupied.

   2 Read a book.

   3 Here's some money, why not go and get a video from Mr Patel?

F. When Snotty has lost something, do you say:
1 It's your own fault. You're always losing things. You'd lose your head, if it wasn't tied on.
2 Now just think back to exactly where you had it last.
3 Don't worry, it'll turn up if you don't think about it.

HAPPY →

G. When Snotty comes home and says he only got 17% for Maths, do you say:
1 I'm surprised you got as much as that, the way you revised.
2 Right, my lad, extra homework from now on.
3 Heh, that's pretty good. Let's go to Marine Ices and celebrate.

UNHAPPY ←

The idea of having some multiple choice questions had been first suggested by Jessie. She said that to interview ten people was going to be very difficult, in fact it could take hours. They needed a simple method of eliminating the useless ones, the out-of-touch, the dum dums, the horribles, the no-hopers, the old bats, the drears, the humourless or those people only doing it for the money.

"They're all doing it for the money," said Bessie.

"Yes, but we want Snotty to have a mother who also cares, someone on his wavelength, someone he can relate to."

"You're sounding like a social worker now," said Sluke.

"Good," said Jessie. "The lucky applicant might have to deal with a social worker, after she's managed to con, I mean impress, a Head Teacher."

Jessie tried her multiple choice questions on the other three, asking them to tick the answers they would like their ideal mother to give. She altered a few words here and there, refining and rearranging them on Snotty's mother's word processor, then printed them out and made ten copies. Finding ten pens which had not dried up and ten unbroken pencils took almost as long as thinking up the questions.

Together, they then agreed on how they would judge the applicants, depending on which answers they ticked. Once again Jessie wrote it all down, so there would be no arguments later about what they had decided and what sort of mum they were looking for:

UNHAPPY

NUMBER ONE answers. Any applicant ticking even one of the Number One answers would immediately be identified as a bossy boots, horrible, yuck-making, totally unfit for the role of anyone's mother, let alone Snotty's mother. Such people would be eliminated at once. Thank you and goodbye.

BORED →

NUMBER TWO answers. These would indicate a certain seriousness, a certain concern, a certain toughness, but

too many of them would count against the applicant.
Thank you, don't ring us, we'll ring you.

HAPPY →

NUMBER THREE answers. These were what Snotty
would want to hear from his mum. A clean sweep of
number threes, and bingo, the job would be filled. Well
done, when can you start?

4

All four of them were on their best behaviour at school
on Friday, especially Snotty and Sluke. Should either of
them be kept in detention then the whole interviewing
process would be ruined. It had been agreed they would
have equal votes, but that Snotty would have the casting
vote in the event of any disagreements.

"I've just realized something," said Sluke, as he and
Snotty ran home, both of them quickly out of puff,
thanks to all those weeks of ice-cream and chips. "If me,
Jessie and Bessie vote for someone you don't like, that
means it's three to one, so that's not fair, if you then
out-vote us."

"Life's not fair," said Snotty.

"You sound like the sort of mum we don't want,"
said Sluke. "Saying things like that . . ."

"I was just joking."

"How will we know if the applicants are joking or
being serious?"

"I'll know," said Snotty. "I always know with my
mum."

There was already a short queue outside Snotty's front door when he got home. Seven out of the ten were sitting on the front steps, some carrying little make-up cases, some a change of clothing. Three of them had been there all the afternoon, as Mrs Cheatham had observed, watching from behind the curtains.

"What's going on?" said Mrs Cheatham, opening her front door the moment she saw Snotty arriving home.

"They're Snotty's groupies," said Sluke. "Now that he's mega famous."

"Ignore him," said Snotty, giving Sluke a thump. "They've come for my mum, that's all."

He'd chosen his words very carefully, so as not to confuse the actresses, who were all listening, hoping to pick up any clues about what might be expected of them.

"She's going to interview them all for a part, is she?" asked Mrs Cheatham. "How exciting!"

Snotty asked the actresses if they could wait a few minutes longer before the auditions started, then he and Sluke went inside.

Five minutes later, Bessie and Jessie arrived. They'd been home first to change out of their school clothes. First they set up a little table in the hall, where Jessie put down a cassette player and laid out the sets of questions, one for each person, to be filled in straightaway, no talking, no conferring, no looking at each other's answers.

Sluke and Snotty got a long bench out of the back garden and dragged it inside, setting it up at the end of the football pitch. This would be where the judges would sit, interviewing the final short list.

Jessie would first eliminate as many of the ten as possible by giving them the multiple choice questions.

At four o'clock exactly Jessie, wearing her best dress and her most grown-up expression, opened the front door and asked all ten of the actresses to come in. She handed each a set of questions and a pen.

"This is stupid," said one. "I hate questionnaires."

"I'm dyslexic," said another.

"My agent never mentioned this," said a third.

"Thank you and goodbye," said Jessie, sharply, putting on her bossiest expression. She had immediately seen that none of the three was suitable. She ushered them to the door, but managed to turn on the charm when she thanked them ever so kindly for turning up.

The other seven were studying the questionnaires. Some were crouching on the hall floor, some sitting on the stairs, some sitting on their make-up cases.

"What a good idea," said one.

"I love questionnaires," said another.

"Cor, this is hard," said a third, opening her case and taking out a cigarette.

"Sorry, no smoking," said Jessie, opening the front door.

"What do you mean?" said the woman, looking angry.

"The part does not call for smoking," said Jessie. "Thank you for coming."

The remaining six settled down to the questions, except for one at the top of the stairs who kept on looking down, hoping to see what the others were writing.

"That's cheating," said Jessie. "Goodbye and thank you."

So that left five.

When they had finished their answers, Jessie took their papers and marked them quickly. One had ticked every first answer, which they had agreed meant instant disqualification. So she was out. Jessie suspected she had not bothered to read the others, she looked so dozy.

One had ticked four first answers out of a possible eight. She looked alert enough, but very grim and serious, the sort who probably agreed with all the first answers, so she was also out.

Now there were three. None of those remaining had ticked any Number One answers, but on the other hand, none had ticked all the Number Three answers. There was all to play for.

"Close your eyes and pick a pencil," said Jessie. She clutched in her hands three broken pencils that she hadn't been able to use.

"Right, you've picked the shortest one, you can come in first. Then you, then you. Is that clear? Right, first one follow me. You two please wait here. You will be called soon. And no listening at the door. Thank you."

Jessie switched on the cassette player on the hall table. Out came the latest Zo-Ee number, featuring Mrs Mudd. This was to relax the two who were waiting and make it harder for them to hear the interviews in the football pitch, just in case they might be tempted to listen under the door. At the same time she had switched on a tape recorder hidden on the stairs, where the two waiting applicants were sitting, to pick up their conversation.

5

The first applicant on the short list was called Maggie. She was short, fat and jolly, and she wore a full-length Laura Ashley skirt. She didn't look a bit like Snotty's real mother, despite the effect produced by her photograph, but she had an amused, inquisitive expression which appealed to Snotty.

"Hello, Maggie!" said Bessie, trying to be friendly. "Thank you for coming."

"Thank you for asking me," replied Maggie, smiling.

"I've got a Christmas question for you first of all," said Snotty. "What's the best way to serve turkey?"

"I'm afraid I'm no good at cooking," said Margaret, giving another smile, not as radiant this time, quickly glancing round the room. She had been to some unusual auditions in her time, but this was one of the strangest settings. However, people often did start by asking trick questions, just to catch you out.

Snotty put a cross against Maggie on his clipboard. He was the only one with a clipboard, taken from his mother's desk, since he was chairman of the Board of Judges.

The Turkey joke was one of his mother's favourites, so old, so pathetic, so unfunny, yet she always laughed at it. Snotty wanted one of his would-be mums at least to offer a silly answer. His real mother always did that, when she didn't know the answer to something.

"I can't even make toast," continued Margaret. "Unless I have a recipe book."

Snotty gave her another cross, not wanting a mother who couldn't cook, but Jessie nudged his arm, whispering that he should use his rubber. It was a joke, dum dum, Maggie was being funny, you're not the only one who can make jokes.

"How much pocket money do you think twelve-year-olds should get?" asked Sluke, trying to appear serious and solemn.

"I don't know," said Maggie. "One pound a week?"

"What time do you think twelve-year-olds should go to bed?" asked Bessie.

"About eight o'clock?" said Maggie.

"If a teacher complains about your son, whose side would you be on?" asked Snotty.

"Goodness," said Maggie. "That is a difficult one."

They all threw various other questions at Maggie, none of them very hard, none of them meant to trick her, but she could answer very few of them.

"Have you any questions for us?" suggested Jessie.

"I'm a bit confused about the part," began Maggie. "Is it for – er – a tele or a film, a play, or what?"

"Thank you," said Jessie. "Could you please wait outside and send in the next one."

Next came Claire, tall, short hair, wearing a boiler suit and high heels. Again, she didn't look like Snotty's mother, or her own photograph, but Snotty was determined not to hold this against her.

"What's the best way to serve turkey?" asked Snotty.

"Excuse me?" said Claire, looking worried.

"Not a bad answer," said Jessie, putting B+ on Snotty's clipboard, the way Miss Eager did on essays, at least on Jessie's essays. Snotty usually got 'See Me' on his, which he maintained meant C.

"Tell me," said Sluke, "how much do you think twelve-year-olds should get as pocket money?"

"It would depend on the financial and socio-cultural circumstances," said Claire, staring into the faces of her four inquisitors, searching for clues. The setting did not worry her, as she liked a confrontational interview, and was used to them, but she would have preferred more information about inner motivation vis-à-vis her character.

"If your son was not invited to his best friend's party, what would your reaction be?" asked Jessie.

"We would have to define first of all the meaning of 'best friend'," said Claire. "Is it a subjective or objective term? A simple value judgement, or based on a long-term one-to-one relationship? In parenting, it is not always viable to . . ."

"Any questions for us?" asked Jessie, bewildered.

"Who is the director going to be, and is it Brook school acting or Stanislavksy?"

"Thank you," said Snotty, yawning. "Next, please."

The last applicant was called Flora. She was of medium size, medium build, with long curly red hair and spectacles. She was even less like Snotty's mother than either of the other two.

"I didn't realize your hair was red," said Snotty, looking at her photograph.

"It can be any colour you like," said Flora, taking off her wig to reveal short blonde hair. "And so can the specs. They came out of a Christmas cracker."

"How much do you think twelve-year-olds should get for pocket money?" asked Sluke.

"Personally, I think all twelve-year-olds should be out earning their own money," said Flora, very solemnly. "Either by going down the coal mines, or pulling ponies along. Failing that, I'm a great believer in them sweeping chimneys."

All four children looked horrified, till Flora burst out laughing. Snotty gave her a big tick. Jessie added an A.

"What about going to bed?" said Bessie. "When should they go?"

"When they're tired," said Flora.

"If your son didn't get invited to his best friend's party," asked Sluke, "what would you do?"

"Hold a party for him the next week – and invite his best friend, and everyone else he's ever known . . ."

They went through all the questions they had asked before, plus a few more, and each time Flora either gave a silly answer which made them laugh or a serious one with which they agreed.

"Any questions for us?" asked Jessie.

"Yeh," said Flora, looking at the goal posts chalked on the wall. "What time does the match start?"

"Oh, we do have one final question," said Snotty as Flora was getting up. "What's the best way to serve turkey?"

"Join the Turkish army," said Flora, walking towards the door. "Boom, boom."

As she reached the door she turned and took an imaginary kick at an imaginary ball, scoring an imaginary goal in off the fridge. She went out into the hall celebrating an imaginary goal.

6

Snotty was standing at the counter in the school secretary's outer office. At a school the size of St Andrew's
Road Comprehensive, even the school secretary has an
outer office. This was as far as most pupils ever got, to
hand in notes, messages or registers, unless they were
being called before the Head for some misdemeanour.

"This way, Mrs Bumstead," said a junior, opening
the door into the secretary's room and pointing to an old
but comfortable-looking sofa and a couple of wooden
chairs.

The school secretary was working on a computer and
looked up only to give a brief but cold nod to Snotty
and then a brief but slightly warmer nod towards the
woman with him.

"Mrs Bumstead?" she said, already ticking the name
on a list beside her.

"Guilty," said Flora.

The school secretary had been at her desk when the
real Mrs Bumstead had first come to school with her son
while in his last term at primary school, but that had
been a year ago. Hundreds of parents had passed through
her room since then, plus thousands of notes, messages,
registers and quite a few naughty pupils.

"Nice class of sofa," said Flora, sitting down. "Just
as comfortable as I remember from last time."

Snotty had explained to Flora that his mother had
been to the school only once, when she and Snotty had
been seen by the Deputy Head. He had carefully briefed
her on Mrs Potter, on the names of his main teachers,

the names of the main buildings, his best friends, but he had not actually mentioned anything about furniture.

"That sofa's new," said the school secretary. "A gift from the Parents' Association. I don't know what we'd do without them."

"Very true," said Flora. "Without parents, where *would* we all be? Non-existent, if you ask me . . ."

The school secretary looked startled, wondering what this parent was talking about. Snotty gave Flora a nudge. He had warned her not to talk unless spoken to directly. That was his well-tried formula for getting through his school life.

Flora was wearing his mother's clothes, complete with one of her floppy hats. This helped to disguise her short-cropped, punk-style blonde hair. She also had on a long-sleeved blouse to hide a tattoo on her upper arm. Even Jessie had not noticed that at the audition. Snotty's mother had not got any tattoos, unless she had acquired one in Africa.

Snotty had briefed Flora on his mother's job, as much as he could, about her film and TV work – something to do with the casting side, as far as he knew. She had gone off suddenly on some secret project in Africa, with some Big Star, to help some sort of Save the World charity.

A little green light lit up on the school secretary's desk. She got up and opened the door into the Head's office.

"This way, Mrs Bumstead," she said.

Mrs Potter was on the phone, giving some instructions, so Flora sat down on a chair in front of the desk while Snotty stood beside her, feeling very small and very worried. He was beginning to sense that Flora was throwing herself into the part rather more whole-heartedly than he had expected. He also did not care for some of her improvisations.

On Mrs Potter's desk were some photographs of children. Flora immediately leaned over and started exclaiming over them, going "Ooh!" and "Ahh!" and "Coo-ee, coo-ee, coo-ee!".

Snotty knew Mrs Potter was a "Mrs", but that had always seemed to him a title, not a marital fact, just as he had called all his primary school teachers "Miss" whether they had been married or not. Sometimes he'd even called the men teachers "Miss".

If he had known any personal details about Mrs Potter, he would have briefed Flora, but he didn't. No, on second thoughts, he would have told her to make no comments or reactions of a personal nature.

Flora was still oohing and ahhing, putting on a range of funny voices, going quite over the top. Snotty gave her a kick on the ankle, hoping she would desist.

"Ooh, cor, luverly, wot a smasher that one is!" cooed

Flora in a joke cockney accent. "Doncha love him?"

Mrs Potter, still on the phone, swivelled round and looked across the desk, wondering who this person was, making all the silly noises.

"Heh, look at this one!" said Flora, now in a deep American accent. "What a hunk."

Mrs Potter put the phone down and picked up some notes in front of her, making sure her five o'clock appointment was with a First Year parent, not some hysterical Sixth Former, suffering from exam fatigue, who had wandered in by mistake.

"Lovely children," said Flora, now affecting a posh English accent. "Are they your own, or rented?"

"What?" said Mrs Potter, still adjusting, putting the phone call from her mind, realizing at last that Flora's pretend kisses were aimed at the photographs on her desk.

"Oh, yes, *les enfants*," said Mrs Potter, smiling. "It is a bit corny, having one's kids on one's desk."

"Oh, it's sweet really," said Flora. "Lots of people do it, in fact I'm thinking of setting up a rent-a-kid business, you know, people who haven't got kids and want to appear caring and loving, they could hire my kids for their family photos. Or say your own kids are horrible and ugly, I could rent you some stunners. Or say your own kids simply refuse to be photographed, which I know a lot of kids do, they can be a pain sometimes, don't you agree, then you could hire my kids, by the hour, by the day, by the metre, well you wouldn't want titchy ones, would you . . ."

"Jolly good idea," said Mrs Potter coldly, glancing at her notes again, and then at Snotty, trying to remember if she had seen him before. He did look rather small, even for a First Year, but he was standing awkwardly,

on one left foot. Had he been injured, she wondered?
The report in front of her did suggest he was not being
properly cared for.

"Then when I've set up that business," continued
Flora, still in full flow, ignoring Mrs Potter's cold stare,
"I might go into rent-a-mum, whatja fink, Mrs P.,
groovy idea, huh? Ever heard of rent-a-mum?"

Snotty glared at Flora. She was now going too far. He
should have signed a contract with her, to play the part
properly, making her responsible if she mucked the

whole thing up. She seemed determined to give things away rather than protect him.

Snotty swung his right foot against her ankles as hard as he could. She gave a yell but managed to grab Snotty's foot and hold on to it, while still talking.

"I have often hired out my own dear Nottingham for photos," said Flora, "in advertising work, and for women's magazines. They often want photographs of the 'surly' child, the obstreperous child, the standing-on-one-foot and glaring child, or even the falling-down-on-the-floor and screaming sort of child . . ."

She let go of Snotty's leg when he least expected it, and he went crashing to the floor.

"Yes, I'm sure there's a call for that sort of thing," said Mrs Potter, checking the report in front of her once again, while Snotty picked himself up.

"You haven't been to a parents' evening yet, have you, Mrs Bumstead?" said Mrs Potter.

"No, and I'm terribly sorry," said Flora, replying in her normal voice at last. "I've meant to each time, and each time it's coincided with panic at work. You know how it is . . ."

"Nor have you managed to see Miss Eager," continued Mrs Potter, "even when she invited you to talk to her informally."

"Guilty again," said Flora, putting on her most demure and humble look.

"The thing is," said Mrs Potter, "Miss Eager has become worried about Nottingham. He has not been handing his homework in on time, his clothes always look unwashed and on occasions he has fallen asleep in class, as if perhaps he has been up all night . . ."

"Ah, the petal," said Flora, giving Snotty an affectionate cuddle. "The thing is, Mrs Potter, speaking mother to mother, which I hope I can, hmm? He's always looked like that!"

Flora smiled, hoping she had softened any further blows or criticisms which might be coming.

"To put it bluntly, Mrs Nottingham," said Mrs Potter, "the signs are that he is being left on his own for long stretches of time."

"On his own?" laughed Flora. "Snotty, I mean Nottingham, is never on his own. He's the most popular boy on the block, always surrounded by loads of friends, the house is always filled with his chums . . ."

"That's what we're concerned about, Mrs Bumstead," said Mrs Potter. "While you are away, which I know you have to be from time to time, because of your work, perhaps he is entertaining too many of his friends?"

"But I love his friends being around," said Flora. "It's only on rare occasions I have to be away, goodness me, then he looks after the place beautifully. Mrs Cheatham, my next-door neighbour, is always saying how kempt our house is. Kempt? Can one say kempt, Mrs Potter? You're the teacher, ha ha."

"That's as may be," said Mrs Potter, frowning at her notes. "But some people are becoming rather concerned."

"Mrs Pratt, by any chance? Well, she was telling me only the other day what a lovely tea he gave her. You do know her, don't you? Social Services. She made a social call. That's why it's called Social Services, boom boom."

"Yes, I know about her call," said Mrs Potter, checking her notes again. "She was not entirely convinced, though she did talk to you on the phone, I believe?"

"She certainly did, and what a lovely conversation we had, but then she is a lovely, caring, wonderful woman!"

"I see she's due to call again next month."

"Oh, I'll be there this time, in the flesh. Every time I'm needed from now on I'll be there, doing my bit, playing my part as a good mother. After all, I need the money . . ."

"What?" said Mrs Potter.

"I mean I need the money from my film work in Africa."

"Yes, I'd heard about that," said Mrs Potter.

"I did think of teaching after I left Sussex," said Flora, "but I knew I wouldn't have the patience."

"Yes, it does take patience," said Mrs Potter, glancing at the clock on the wall. "Among other things."

"Unlike some forms of women's work," said Flora, lowering her voice, becoming confidential, "mine goes in short, sharp bursts. With you, Mrs Potter, I'm sure it must be intense all the time. What problems you must have to cope with, education in crisis, schools under such pressures, opting in, opting out, opting all over the jolly old place! I suspect you hardly see your own dear children during the week, hmm? Hence these lovely photographs on your desk . . ."

Flora picked up the photographs again, but this time she looked at them quietly and solemnly, shaking her head and sighing.

"Working women can so easily miss the best years in their children's lives. So sad, so difficult."

"We all have to make sacrifices," said Mrs Potter briskly.

"Yes, and that often means, from time to time, in little ways, we may neglect our own children," said Flora. "Don't you think, hmm?"

"There is neglect and neglect . . ."

"Any neglect I've been guilty of, and I'm willing to admit it, is now over. The film I'm working on is nearly finished. If you're very good, I'll invite you to the première. How about that, eh, Mrs P.?"

Flora stood up and put one arm round Snotty, smiling broadly. Snotty tried to force out a smile, sensing that Flora had come to some sort of climax in her performance. Then he forced it in again. He remembered he'd taken a vow of non-smiling while on school premises.

"It will be a royal première, will it?" said Mrs Potter with a knowing smile. "Using your royal contacts, of course."

For a moment, Flora looked blank. She felt she'd given a star performance, but here was a line she didn't quite know how to follow.

Oh no, thought Snotty. How could he have forgotten to tell Flora about the Royal visitation? Mrs Potter must have heard about it, perhaps even seen the letter he'd copied. What if Flora now denied having any Royal friends?

"Ah, the Royals," said Flora, thinking hard. "I'll introduce you to some of the Royals I've known all my life."

"That'll be nice," said Mrs Potter, standing up.

"The Grand Old Duke of York," said Flora. "He'll be there, if he's not marching! Old King Cole – we need him there, just to be merry. Boom boom. The Queen of Hearts – she'll be doing some baking for the party afterwards. And if the King in his Counting House can get away, he'll be there as well. It is a children's film, after all . . ."

"Sounds delightful," said Mrs Potter. She shook hands with Flora, signalling that the interview was over.

Then Mrs Potter did a strange thing, something out of character. As Snotty was leaving the room, she gently ruffled his hair. It felt sticky. Had it not been washed for a long time? That was often a sign of neglect. No, it must be some new shampoo.

After they had left the room, Mrs Potter smelt her hand. A mixture of honey and tomato ketchup. Funny shampoo!

7

The next morning, Sluke and Snotty slept in very late. They had been out the evening before, celebrating at Marine Ices with Bessie and Jessie. Then he and Sluke had stayed up most of the night, playing football and watching videos.

"Look at the time," said Sluke, waking up Snotty. He'd got up first and been down to get the last of the tomato ketchup and honey ice-cream. "Gerrup. Flora will be here for her wages at eleven o'clock. Have you got enough cash for her?"

"Don't panic," said Snotty. "I've got plenty."

"Where do you keep it?" asked Sluke.

"Mind your own business," said Snotty.

"I think you should pay her double. She did a great job!"

"Huh, she nearly didn't," said Snotty. "My leg still hurts where she held on to me."

"So that's why you were useless at football last night."

"Yeh, but I still beat you, so there."

"It solves all our problems from now on," said Sluke. "Having Flora as a rent-a-mum. It was a great idea of mine."

"Liar. I thought of it," said Snotty. "I think of everything."

"Well, think of a new ice-cream we can make today. It's your turn."

They went downstairs together. Sluke looked in the fridge, hoping there might be some drinks or other delicacies which he had missed on his dawn raid. The shelves were practically empty, as they were going shopping later, but the freezing compartment looked almost overflowing. Snotty had told him it was full of kidneys and liver, left by his mother.

"Yuck, what a rotten fridge," said Sluke, slamming the door.

"Don't do that, you idiot," shouted Snotty. "I need to get in there. Now I'll have to wait."

"Oh, no, you're not going to make kidney and liver ice-cream, are you? Ugh. Disgusting."

"Heh, not a bad suggestion," said Snotty. "Wish I'd thought of that. You've got a brain cell or two still functioning."

Snotty opened the freezer part and took out a large plastic bag, frozen solid. He held it under the hot tap for five minutes to let it melt. Out of it he drew a bundle of ten pound notes, enough to pay Flora, the milkman and for the Saturday shopping.

"Another of my great ideas," said Snotty.

8

Flora arrived bang on time to collect her wages. She had a skinhead haircut this time, which appeared to be real unless it was a skinhead wig. She didn't seem at all concerned that some of her bank notes were still cold and stiff.

"Better than handling hot money," she said. "I've been given some of that in my time, I can tell you, from dodgy agents."

As she was counting out her money, the phone rang so she picked it up, still considering she was working, despite her haircut.

"Zoe Bumstead speaking," she said. "Who's that?"

"Zoe Bumstead," said a faint voice at the other end. The line was poor and crackling.

"Excuse me," said Flora, putting on one of her silly

voices. "You must have the wrong person, if not the wrong planet. Who are you, where are you, and why are you saying you are me?"

"I'm ringing from Africa," said the voice. "What's going on? I'd like to speak to Snotty . . ."

Flora put her hand over the phone and beckoned to Snotty.

"Oh, no, it must be her," she hissed. "Your real mum."

"Hello," said Snotty, picking up the phone. "Mum?"

"Who else did you think it was?" said his mother. "Old Mother Hubbard? Who was that who picked up the phone?"

"Oh, er, it was Jessie, just being silly."

"Listen, this is just a quick call, only a few seconds," said his mother. "I'm just about to get a boat into the Okavango delta, can't tell you any more details, but this is to say I'm fine and hope you're getting on OK, doing your school work, washing your face, and your hair, and it won't be long now before I'm back, love you, Snotty face . . ."

The phone went dead, just as the front door bell rang. Flora went to answer it.

Snotty sat down, half dazed, rather stunned, but very thrilled to have heard from his mother.

"Good gracious, what an amazing surprise," said Flora at the front door. "This is incredible."

Snotty groaned. He could hear Flora exclaiming and shouting, roaring and laughing. He presumed it was one of her silly tricks so he sent Sluke down the hall to see what was happening, if anything.

Flora was in the arms of the milkman, holding on to him, shrieking and giggling.

"After all these years," she said. "We meet again."

126

"Yeh, isn't it amazing?" said the milkman.

"What's going on?" said Sluke.

"We were at university together," said Flora, clinging to the milkman. "My first feller! And he's just as hunky as ever."

"Huh," said Sluke, looking rather embarrassed. "I'll tell Snotty you're here."

Sluke took the milk, sugar and eggs, and went back to the football pitch. Snotty was still sitting on the floor, thinking about his mother's phone call, a happy smile on his face. Sluke told him what had happened.

"Where's the milkman's money?" said Sluke. "I'll pay him."

"No, I'll do it," said Snotty.

Snotty went into the hall followed by Sluke, but there was no sign of the milkman or Flora. Then, through the open front door they saw the milkman sitting in his milk float. Beside him was Flora, her arm round him. There was a burst of peeping on the horn and then the milk float set off, straight down the street, ignoring several neighbours who had been waiting for their delivery.

"I wonder if I'll ever see my rent-a-mum again," said Snotty, closing the door, putting the milkman's money back in his pocket. "Don't suppose it matters. I'll be having my real mum home soon. I hope . . ."